RED GOODWIN

OTHER BOOKS BY JOHN WILSON

Young Adult Fiction

Weet, 1995, Napoleon Publishing
Weet's Quest, 1997, Napoleon Publishing
Weet Alone, 1995, Napoleon Publishing
Across Frozen Seas, 1997, Beach Holme Publishing
Ghosts of James Bay, 2001, Beach Holme Publishing
Lost in Spain, 2000, Fitzhenry & Whiteside
Adrift in Time, 2003, Ronsdale Press
And in the Morning, 2003, Kids Can Press
Flames of the Tiger, 2003, Kids Can Press
Flags of War, 2004, Kids Can Press
Battle Scars, 2005, Kids Can Press
Four Steps to Death, 2005, Kids Can Press

Young Adult Non-fiction

Norman Bethune: A Life of Passionate Conviction,
1999, XYZ Publishing
John Franklin: Traveller on Undiscovered Seas, 2001, XYZ Publishing
Righting Wrongs: The Story of Norman Bethune,
2001, Napoleon Publishing
Discovering the Arctic: The Story of John Rae, 2003, Napoleon Publishing
*Dancing Elephants and Floating Continents: The Story of Canada Beneath
Your Feet,* 2003, Key Porter Publishing

Adult Fiction

North with Franklin: The Lost Journals of James Fitzjames,
1999, Fitzhenry & Whiteside

Red Goodwin

John Wilson

RONSDALE PRESS

RED GOODWIN
Copyright © 2006 John Wilson

RONSDALE PRESS
3350 West 21st Avenue, Vancouver, B.C., Canada V6S 1G7
www.ronsdalepress.com

Typesetting: Julie Cochrane, in Minion 12 pt on 16
Front Cover Photo: Union Camp, near Cumberland, c. 1888. Courtesy of
    Cumberland Museum.
Back Cover Photo: Ginger Goodwin, c. 1916. Courtesy of Cumberland Museum.
Cover Design: Julie Cochrane
Paper: Ancient Forest Friendly Rolland "Enviro" — 100% post-consumer
    waste, totally chlorine-free and acid-free

Ronsdale Press wishes to thank the Canada Council for the Arts, the Government of Canada through the Book Publishing Industry Development Program (BPIDP), and the Province of British Columbia through the British Columbia Arts Council for their support of its publishing program.

Library and Archives Canada Cataloguing in Publication

Wilson, John (John Alexander), 1951–
    Red Goodwin / John Wilson.

    ISBN-10: 1-55380-034-6
    ISBN-13: 978-1-55380-034-7

    1. Goodwin, Albert, 1887–1918 — Juvenile fiction. 2. Coal mines and
mining — British Columbia — Cumberland — Juvenile fiction.
3. Cumberland (B.C.) — Juvenile fiction. I. Title.

PS8595.I5834R43 2006   jC813'.54   C2006-900023-9

At Ronsdale Press we are committed to protecting the environment. To this end we are working with Markets Initiative (www.oldgrowthfree.com) and printers to phase out our use of paper produced from ancient forests. This book is one step towards that goal.

Printed in Canada by Marquis Printing, Quebec

This one's for Chris and Paul.
A lot of these words are here because of them.

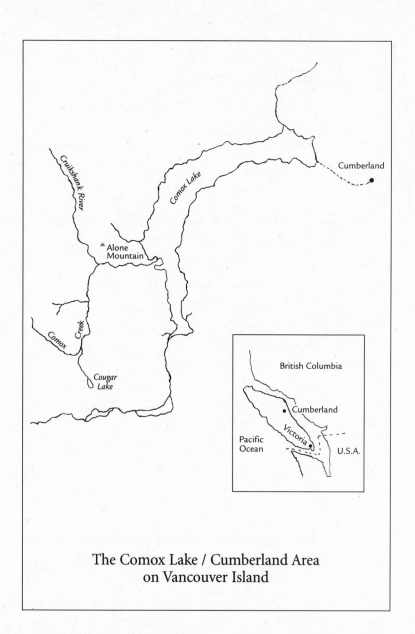

The Comox Lake / Cumberland Area
on Vancouver Island

Saturday, January 27, 1968

—⁓—

The bitter rain, carried on the frigid blast that sweeps off the ice caps on Forbidden Plateau, slashes across the lonely graveyard. The raindrops, cold enough almost to be snow, sting my exposed cheeks and the wind cuts through my overcoat. I envy my family, Ted, Dolores and little Rafael, sitting, snug in the warm, fog-windowed car by the cemetery gates. They offered to accompany me, but this is a journey I must take on my own.

Whenever I visit this cemetery, even in the freezing rain, I walk along the rows of headstones, across and back, up and down, past the occupants of this small city of the dead. Some of the names I recognize and hesitate at: Bill Ward,

Jimmy Wong, my aunt and uncle, Charles and Sophie Ryan, and my first love, Morag McLean. Each has a tale to tell — some mysterious, some exciting, some sad — but only one story here changed my life. It is a story of the summer of 1918, when I was sixteen. The summer when the Great War was four years old, the Russian Czar and his family were shot, the great influenza epidemic began and the first air-mail service started. But my story doesn't deal with those world-shaking events. It is about a lake, a dozen square miles of forest and the lives of a few ordinary people that intersected one hot July week all those years ago.

I step up to an irregular, rough block of reddish sand-stone and wipe the rain from my glasses. Below a blood-red, crudely carved hammer and sickle, I read the stark, angry words:

LEST WE FORGET
GINGER GOODWIN
SHOT JULY 26TH
1918
A WORKERS FRIEND

Apart from the missing apostrophe, there are two mis-takes on the headstone. The hammer and sickle shouldn't be there. The man who lies below the symbol wasn't a Com-munist — there wasn't even a Communist party in Canada when he lived. It was added when the gravestone was erected in the thirties and the Communists were looking for heroes.

The date is wrong too. Ginger wasn't shot on July 26. It was July 27, another Saturday. I doubt if many visitors notice that. I know only because I was there that day almost half a century ago.

I shiver and pull my coat tighter about me, but it makes no difference. It is not the cold that is making me shiver, it is the past.

Saturday, July 20, 1918

AFTERNOON

—◦◦◦—

"You cannot separate the war in the trenches of France from the war being fought in the coal mines of British Columbia. Both are inevitable the way the world is set up at the moment. The soldiers in the trenches — British, French, German, and Canadian — are being fooled by their governments. The miners are being fooled by the company, and long hours and unsafe practices are killing miners as surely as German bombs and bullets are killing soldiers in Flanders."

The man standing on the tree stump was not tall and there was a wiry thinness to him beneath his threadbare jacket and trousers. He held his arms wide before him and his clean-shaven face bore an expression of intense concentration. He spoke with a distinct English accent — Lancashire, I guessed — and his words made my blood boil. How dare this deserter compare what was going on here in this remote corner of the British Empire to the struggle in France that had taken my father's life? How dare he compare my father to a German soldier?

"The difference is that in France it is worker fighting against worker, on Vancouver Island it is worker fighting against boss."

I could barely prevent myself from leaping up and calling the man a cowardly liar. What stopped me was fear. I had never set eyes on him before, but I recognized him. The shock of fiery red hair above his pale face told me who this was: Red Goodwin.

Despite being in the town of Cumberland only a bare two months, I had heard his name countless times. It was on everyone's lips, either as a curse or a prayer. To the workers he was a saint, the man who had helped lead the Big Strike of 1912–1914, the man who had led the smelter strike in Trail, the man who fought tirelessly for workers' rights and was being hounded mercilessly by the police for doing so. To my uncle and the mine bosses, he was a dangerous revolutionary, intent upon bringing down the establishment, destroying all property, and plunging Canada into red revolution. To the government he was a draft dodger, a deserter who was hiding in the woods and for whom dozens of Special Policemen were searching.

"I ask you, comrades: Which struggle is more worthwhile? Which struggle will change the world for the better? Which struggle is more just?"

The man emphasized each point by pounding the empty air with a clenched fist. After the final question, Goodwin paused as if to give the crowd an opportunity to answer or to roar its approval. But the scattered stumps that formed his audience were silent.

It was almost funny, this ragged orator passionately declaiming to an audience of dead trees. If it hadn't been for what he was saying, I would have laughed out loud. It was also, despite what he was saying, oddly comforting to hear a familiar English accent after the numbing variety of foreign voices I had heard since I had arrived: Italian, American, Eastern European, Chinese. In fact, it had been the familiarity of the voice that had drawn me here. I had heard the speech long before I had seen its owner and crawled unobserved to the point where I could now watch closely.

Goodwin was drawing to a conclusion. "Comrades! Let us finish this meeting by singing the Red Flag."

The tree stumps remained silent but Goodwin, waving his arms as if conducting a choir, burst into song. His voice was thin and didn't carry a tune well but there was obvious passion in the words:

The people's flag is deepest red
It shrouded oft our martyred dead
And ere their limbs grew stiff and cold
Their hearts' blood dyed its every fold

Then raise the scarlet standard high
Within its shade we'll live and die
Though cowards flinch and traitors sneer
We'll keep the red flag flying here

With heads uncovered swear we all
To bear it onward 'till we fall
Come dungeons dark or gallows grim
This song shall be our parting hymn

Then raise the scarlet standard high . . .

In his enthusiasm to pull a tune from his mute audience, Goodwin, forgetting he was on a narrow stump, stepped forward. The rotting wood at the edge crumbled beneath his weight and he crashed awkwardly to the ground. The song died in a cry of pain. Instinctively, I jumped up to help.

When I reached him, Goodwin was already beginning to pull himself to his feet. Seeing me, he stopped. A look of utter embarrassment crossed his face, then he burst out laughing, showing several gold-crowned teeth. His laugh was deeper than his slight body suggested. I hesitated, conflicting feelings rushing through me. My fear had gone. How could a laughing man who sang to tree stumps be dangerous? But my anger was still there, balanced by the instinct that had made me rush to help him. As I watched, his laugh seemed to catch in his throat, deteriorating into a harsh, shuddering cough that threatened to tear his frame apart.

Scrabbling in his pocket, Goodwin produced a grubby handkerchief and held it to his mouth. Leaning back, he rested against the stump. I was horrified to see the handkerchief flecked with spots of fresh blood. Goodwin saw me staring at the rag and hurriedly crumpled it up and returned it to his pocket. Then he smiled at me.

"So I had an audience after all. These hills are becoming too busy for a man to practise his oratory in peace and solitude. And what might your name be?"

"Will," I answered hesitantly. "Will Ryan."

"Will Ryan," repeated Goodwin thoughtfully. "Well, Will, my name is Albert," he went on, holding out his hand for me to shake. I ignored it. "My friends call me Ginger, on account of my hair. My enemies call me much worse, on account of my politics."

"I know. You're Red Goodwin."

"Yes," he acknowledged with a slight nod. "That is one of the politer names I am called. You look well-dressed for a miner's son. Might you be related to Charles Ryan, mine manager down at the Number Four pit?"

"He's my uncle," I answered, "my father's brother." Mention of my father reminded me of my anger. "What right do you have to talk about the men fighting over in France. You're a damned deserter."

Goodwin regarded me quietly for a moment, pondering my outburst. "Well," he said at length, "damned I might be, but it's arguable whether I am a deserter, since I have never joined anyone's army. The government simply chose to assign me a number when I didn't show up in answer to the Military Service Act." Goodwin straightened his back, saluted and said, "Private Albert Goodwin, number 270432, Number 2 Depot Battalion, Victoria, currently absent without leave, at your service." Then he slouched back. "Is your father in the army?"

"He was," I said bitterly. "He was a captain. He was killed at Passchendaele last year." I could feel tears welling behind my eyes. "So don't you insult him!"

Goodwin raised his hand in supplication. "I'm sorry," he said. "I meant no disrespect to your father. You must miss him terribly. I have not seen my father since I boarded the *City of Bombay* in Liverpool, these twelve years past."

"But he is still alive!"

"True, if you consider an existence in the West Riding Lunatic Asylum, struggling to draw air into coal-blackened lungs a life.

"It is good to be angry, young Will, but be careful to direct your anger at those who deserve it."

We looked at each other in silence for a long time. Images of my father flooded my mind — playing cricket with me in the garden, carving the Christmas turkey at the dining table, taking me fishing, playing cards and board games in the parlour or reading while I played with my lead soldiers on the carpet.

"Where did you grow up, Will?"

"In Yorkshire," I replied. "Near to Whitby on the coast. My father was a veterinarian."

Goodwin nodded. "And you lived in a house that stood on its own surrounded by a small garden where you played. Perhaps there was a small stream nearby where you fished. The house had a dining room where you ate family meals and you had your own bedroom. The parlour had a piano and a gramophone where you spent most evenings, you playing on the floor while your father read and your mother sewed."

"My mother died when I was two. I don't remember her."

"I am sorry to hear that. Were you close to one of the servants?"

"Yes, Emily, the cook. She used to talk to me while she worked in the kitchen and pass me pieces of her fudge, hot from the tin."

"And there was running water in the kitchen and indoor toilets."

I nodded, amazed at how accurately Goodwin had recreated my childhood home. "How do you know all this?"

"Because, Will, you are a product of your class. Your accent, attitude and father's profession betray you."

I began to protest, but Goodwin continued. "You had no choice. None of us do. All we can attempt is to see past the restrictions we are born into.

"I too was born in the north of England, but into a different class. My father was a hewer, he worked at the coal face. We moved a lot, but I grew up mostly near Conisbrough.

"I've been there," I interrupted excitedly. "We went to see the castle. It was built in 1100."

"And a beautiful spot it is too, but we lived on the other side of the river, in Denaby Main. We had a four-room house on Firbeck Street."

"That's not too small. Our house only had six rooms."

"And how many of you lived in it?"

"Father and I — if you don't count Emily who slept in the attic. The gardener lived in the village."

Goodwin smiled. "There were twelve of us in our house before my older brothers moved away. But we were lucky."

"How?" I asked, struggling to imagine what those cramped conditions must have been like.

"To have so many survive. More than a quarter of the children in Denaby Main died before they reached their first birthday. Not having room for the piano in the parlour was a small price to pay.

"We fetched our water from two taps along the street and had to go out the back to the privy, which was just a hole in the ground that was shovelled out each night. I could never decide whether it was worse going out in the winter to freeze or in the summer to choke on the smell and the flies."

"That's terrible. Couldn't anyone do anything?"

"They could, but it was too expensive for the mine owners to spend money just on workers' comforts and health. The more workers they could cram into cheap housing close to the mine, the more profitable it was for them.

"That was why I came over here in '06. I heard stories of wide open spaces and that sounded better than Denaby Main."

Goodwin laughed and swung his arm to encompass the desolate view. "I certainly have enough wide open spaces now."

The mention of the wilderness and why Goodwin was living out here, snapped me back to reality and reminded me of my anger. "I have to go," I said abruptly.

"Very well," said Goodwin. "I am glad to have met you, Will Ryan, and I hope we shall meet again."

I turned and hurried back into the bush and down the narrow path that led to the river and the spot where I had cached my fishing rod and catch when I had first heard the voice in the wilderness. I sat on a rock and gazed out over the rippling water. I was horribly confused. All the emotions I had been keeping in check since I had stepped off the boat at Union Bay back in the middle of May, broke free. I wept.

When I eventually calmed down, I felt better, but there was still much I didn't understand. The man I had just met didn't fit the picture my uncle presented of a rabid revolutionary bent on murdering all of us in our beds. And why were the police so keen on capturing him for refusing to go and fight in France? It was obvious he was too sick to fight anywhere. I knew what the blood spots on the handkerchief meant — consumption. Even if I hated what he said about the soldiers in France, I couldn't wish that fate on him. Red Goodwin was dying without facing German bullets.

As insects buzzed around me in the warm summer air, my mind spun back over my long, strange journey to this remote place. It had begun almost a year ago in a different world.

—⁓—

In 1916, when my father had first gone overseas with his regiment, Emily had been let go and the house outside Whitby closed up. Reluctantly, I moved inland to stay in the tiny village of Little Crakehall with my grandparents. They were old and boring and very strict but, since they had scant time for an active boy, I was given the run of the house, the village and the surrounding countryside. I filled my days with school work and my spare hours with fishing and rambling, but the nights were bad. That was when I had too much time to think and missed my father most. I had his letters from the war and his one, glorious leave, but a horrible loneliness crept into my room as the sun went down each evening. Then, last autumn — it was Monday, October the fifteenth — the telegram arrived and my world collapsed. That winter was the worst of my life.

In March of this year, just when I was beginning to believe that life might be worth living again, I was called through to my grandfather's study. I entered nervously and took a seat in front of a huge desk amidst book-lined walls. The room smelled of leather and pipe tobacco and I vividly remember the glass-like shine on the desk's dark surface. My grandfather was obviously nervous and spent some time filling and tamping his curved pipe. At last he lit the pipe, cleared his throat and peered at me from beneath his bushy, white eyebrows.

"I know this has not been an easy year for you," he said in his gruff voice.

I nodded mutely.

"Your father's death in the service of his country was a blow for all of us. We have been happy to put you up while your father was away, but you cannot stay here indefinitely."

He had my total attention now. What had they planned for me?

The old man cleared his throat once more and continued awkwardly. "Uhm, you are aware that you have an uncle in Canada?"

I nodded again — Uncle Charles, my father's younger brother. I had never met him. He and my Aunt Sophie had emigrated before I was born, but we had heard he had done quite well for himself — he apparently owned a mine in western Canada and wrote letters home about the big house they lived in and all the important people they met when they went down to the provincial capital, Victoria.

"Well," my grandfather went on, taking a puff of his pipe, "he has offered to look after you, and we feel that it would be for the best."

I was stunned. As far as I had thought about it, I had assumed that I would go on living with my grandparents. The possibility of being farmed out to some remote corner of the colonies had never even occurred to me.

"What?" was all I could manage to say.

"Now, your Uncle Charles," grandfather elaborated, encouraged that he had got over the most difficult part of his speech, "is quite well off by all accounts. He and your Aunt Sophie have no children, so there will be plenty of room for you. We think that a new start in the New World would be just the thing to help you get over this tragedy."

"No!" I shouted.

My grandfather looked startled.

"I won't go. You can't pack me off to some God-forsaken wilderness, just because I am an orphan now. Father would never have allowed it."

Grandfather looked uncomfortable for a moment, but he soon recovered his gruff authority. "Now see here," he said, stabbing the air with the stem of his pipe, "the decision has been made. Much thought has gone into it and it is in your best interests. Your father was not a rich man. The house at Whitby will be sold and some of the proceeds sent to cover your upkeep in Canada. The remainder will be put in trust until you are twenty-one. Your ticket has been purchased. You sail from Liverpool for Vancouver in two weeks. We will provide money for the journey and we will wire some to your uncle to see to your needs until the house sells. That is an end to it. Good luck."

There was to be no discussion. My life had been decided and I could only follow the path prepared for me.

The following days were hectic as I wrestled with what was happening and struggled to pack my entire life into a single steamer trunk. In contrast, the ocean voyage was sedate and boring in the extreme. The only highlights were travelling on the new canal through Panama and a stopover in the vibrant city of San Francisco.

I loved my three days in San Francisco. For the first time in my life I was free with no one to tell me what to do. I explored the wharves and hilly streets of the city, recently rebuilt after the terrible earthquake and fire of 1906. Everywhere people were friendly and no one cared that I was a kid. I particularly enjoyed the colourful, exotic bustle of Chinatown. It was wonderful after the restrictions of my grandfather's house and I promised myself that I would return one day.

In contrast, Vancouver was dirty and noisy. It seemed as if it were still being carved out of the wilderness. I also lacked freedom there. No sooner had I descended the gangway when I came face-to-face with a Chinese boy of about my age. He was shorter than me and dressed in western clothes. He carried a wooden sign with my name painted on it in red and he looked as though he didn't want to be there.

"You young Ryan?" he asked, as I hesitated before him. He spoke perfect English, unlike the sing-song dialect I had struggled to understand in San Francisco.

"Yes."

"Good. I'm Jimmy Wong. Now hurry up and collect your trunk. We've got a ship to catch."

As we pushed through the crowd of disembarking passengers, I tried to engage my guide in conversation. "Is my uncle Charles too busy to come over himself?"

"He's a boss," Jimmy threw back over his shoulder. "Bosses are always too busy."

"Do you work in his house?"

Jimmy let out a snort of laughter, but remained silent.

I persevered. "You speak very good English."

Jimmy stopped and spun around. "You mean, I no speaky like other Chink men?"

The bitterness in his voice took me aback. "I didn't mean . . . I wasn't . . ." I tried desperately to apologize.

"Look, I doubt if there were many orientals where you come from, so I will explain. For starters, I'm only half Chinese. My mother's white. My father is the shift foreman for the Chinese labourers at the mine your uncle manages. But I look full Chinese and, over here, that makes me the lowest of the low. For a third of the money a white miner is paid, the Chinese are allowed to do the lousy, dangerous jobs that no one else will do — and we have to pay a head tax for the privilege. It doesn't matter if a man's a famous Confucian philosopher in China, in the coal mines he's a Chink, fit only to be given a number and told where to shovel coal.

"Cumberland's a small town and the school's even smaller. We'll run into each other, but that doesn't mean we have anything in common. I'm Chinese, you're white. I'm the son of a worker, you're the nephew of a boss. You keep your upper class attitudes for high tea and I'll get on with my life."

Jimmy turned and began pushing through the crowd. I was confused by his outburst, but I was angry as well. I grabbed him by the shoulder. "You don't know me! You're guilty of exactly what you accuse the whites here of doing, assuming I am what your prejudices tell you I should be.

"All right, there weren't any Chinese where I grew up. Is that my fault? I know nothing about this place and, believe me, I would rather not be here, but I'm just as stuck as you are. Label me the boss's nephew if you want, but don't assume that makes me the same as him."

Jimmy stared hard at me as the crowd surged around us. Then a smile creased his face and he burst out laughing. "Fair enough. I won't judge you, at least until you've had a chance to find your feet. But you have to promise me something."

"What?"

"You'll invite me to high tea."

Now it was my turn to laugh. "I hate high tea."

"Then, maybe I'll invite you for Dim Sum. But right now we have to catch that steamer to Union Bay."

Jimmy and I didn't talk much on the ship over to Vancouver Island. He seemed content to stand by the rail staring at the densely wooded hills slipping by. I was content to stare at the girl who had met us as we struggled up the gangway with my trunk.

Jimmy had introduced the girl as Morag McLean, a friend of his from school, proving that there were exceptions to his rule of Chinese and whites not getting along. She had taken the opportunity of Jimmy being sent over to collect me, to come and buy some material for her mother.

The instant I set eyes on Morag, I fell madly in love. She was almost as tall as me and staggeringly beautiful. Her face was dominated by a pair of the widest, deepest, dark grey eyes I had ever seen and topped by a luxurious mane of jet black hair. Her parents were Scottish, from the Highlands, and had come over when Morag had been a toddler. She still retained a trace of the lilting accent of her home country and it sent shivers down my spine whenever she talked to me. Unfortunately, that wasn't often. Only once did Morag respond to my stumbling attempts to open conversation. Jimmy had gone for a walk around the deck and I asked if she and he were in the same class at school. Morag laughed, a light, sparkling sound that made my knees weak.

"There is only one room at the school," she explained, "and one teacher, Miss Criche. So everyone, from infants to Jimmy and I, are in one class."

"Isn't that very confusing?" I asked.

"Sometimes. Jimmy and I spend a lot of time helping out the wee ones, but it works quite well — and there is no choice."

"The school can't be very large."

"It isn't. There are only about thirty of us altogether, mostly younger, Jimmy and I are the only seniors."

"Why only two of you?"

"Most boys Jimmy's age are working down the mines and most girls my age are either helping their mothers at home or married. There are not many choices in Cumberland."

"Why are you two still there?"

"I am, because my father thinks an education will make me less Chinese." Jimmy had returned from his walk and stood behind me. "He thinks all Chinese can become just like everyone else here if we wear western clothes, learn to speak good English and get an education. I don't agree, but I can't think of anything else to do, so I stay at school." Jimmy leaned on the rail and watched Vancouver Island draw closer.

"And I haven't yet met anyone that I want to spend my life scrubbing the kitchen floor and laundering underwear for."

"Why don't you leave?"

Morag laughed again, but this time there was a hard, bitter edge to it. "Perhaps you haven't noticed, but Jimmy is Chinese and I'm a woman. Neither are characteristics that help us make an independent way in the world.

"I suppose you'll spend a year or two living with your uncle and then leave to seek fortune and fame. That's what is understood — everyone would be horrified if you decided to work at the coalface. We have roles to fill as well. Jimmy is expected to go down the mine and I'm expected to marry and devote myself to raising as many children as survive. The difference is that you could go and work down the mine. It's far easier to move down the social scale than up."

Morag turned away and joined Jimmy watching the view. I fell silent, shocked by the anger that had suddenly infused what Morag was saying. I had met only two people from Cumberland, and already I felt confused and out of my depth.

I joined my companions staring at the coastline. It looked unutterably wild and dangerous compared to the peaceful, tamed countryside I was used to in England. Visions of huge bears and vicious mountain lions lurking behind the impenetrable curtain of giant trees haunted me. What was awaiting me through the screen of trees?

Uncle Charles met us at the steamship dock. He gave me a gruff hug, but never even thanked Jimmy for collecting me. Morag he dismissed with an, "I didn't know you were going over too."

On the train to Cumberland, Jimmy and Morag sat separately and talked in low voices. I sat with my uncle. After the usual platitudes about my father dying for his country and a few questions about my grandparent's health, he fell silent. I looked out the window. Huge areas of dead tree stumps were everywhere. Dirt roads cut through the forests, and ramshackle collections of rough wooden cabins seemed to be fighting to maintain an existence against the encroaching trees.

Cumberland was better, but only just. It looked like the pictures of cowboy towns I had seen in the western novels I sometimes read or the moving picture shows at the biograph. The main street was dirt, with wooden pavements, or boardwalks as I quickly learned to call them. Some of the false-front buildings were quite large, two or three storeys, but it was a sign of how low my expectations had fallen that I was relieved to see telephone lines running down poles on the street.

My first view of Uncle Charles' house on Penrith Avenue reinforced the suspicion that had been growing in my mind as we progressed through the wilderness, that he had not been altogether truthful in his letters to my grandfather. Sitting amid a row of similar buildings, it certainly dwarfed the miners' cottages I had seen on the edge of town, but it was nothing compared to grandfather's home.

The building was square and surrounded on three sides by a wide verandah. The main floor boasted a formal reception room, dining room, office and kitchen, all of modest size. Upstairs were two bedrooms and a bathroom. The decorations and fittings were comfortable enough, but much of the furniture was worn and out of date. The small garden, that was lovingly tended by my Aunt Sophie, was only a postage stamp compared to the estate my grandfather managed.

Nevertheless, I wasn't to live in town for long. Like many people, as soon as the hot summer weather arrived, Uncle Charles and Aunt Sophie left the Chinese servants in charge and moved out to their cabin on the shores of nearby Comox Lake. Most of the cabins on the lakeshore were rough-and-ready, thrown together from local scraps of wood and tar-paper. Some, farther up the lake, were only tents or lean-tos which provided temporary shelter from the rain squalls that slipped off the surrounding mountains. Most cooking and other activities were done outside and there was always a noisy collection of assorted children splashing in the cold water near the shore.

Our cabin lay a half mile up the lake from the Number Four mine and was a more permanent dwelling than most, with a wood-burning cook stove inside. The front door led off a narrow porch overlooking the lake, directly into a large kitchen/sitting room. Behind this were two bedrooms, the smaller of which was mine.

I adapted rapidly to the informal life of the cabin. The only difficulty was that there was no indoor plumbing. Water for washing and cooking was taken directly from the lake and there was a wooden outhouse in the trees at the back. The outhouse, with its plank of wood balanced over a deep hole in the ground, took some getting used to, but there was no choice and, eventually, I barely noticed the smell.

My uncle didn't own the Number Four mine as he had given the family in England to believe; he only managed it. The mine was one of several in the area that had been started by Robert Dunsmuir, a bitter old Scotsman who had built a gloomy castle in Victoria. After he had died, his son James took over the mines and sold them for a huge profit to Consolidated Coal (Dunsmuir) Ltd. The new owners also lived in Victoria and didn't care what happened two hundred miles away as long as the mine kept making a profit. So my Uncle Charles had almost complete control of the day-to-day running of the mine. This made him an important man in the town, but it didn't make him popular.

Uncle Charles was one of the bosses, and as Goodwin had said on his tree stump, there was a war going on between the workers and the bosses. Of course, Uncle Charles' views on the struggle were different from Goodwin's. The workers were wrong. They didn't realize how tough it was to sell coal with war disrupting trade and oil slowly competing with the black rock. To Uncle Charles, they should be grateful that there was work at all and understand that strikes and so forth were in nobody's interests. He reserved special venom for Goodwin and other socialist union organizers.

"That man Goodwin," he would say, his thumbs hooked on the pockets of his waistcoat, "and those like him will stop at nothing short of red revolution. If he is not stopped he will destroy this country just as the Bolsheviks are destroying Russia. He is a traitor to all the brave soldiers fighting and dying in France and he cares nothing for any of the values that are important to this country. All he craves is power — the power to rule over the smoking ruins of everything that sensible men and women hold dear."

Uncle Charles was not one to mince words and was very clear in his views. This was different from my father who was always open to another perspective, but maybe that was just because of where they lived. Out here in the Canadian wilderness it was a land of extremes. Extremes of nature and extremes of ideas. It was taking me quite some time to get used to it.

And now I had met Red Goodwin. It was actually only a few days since I had arrived but it seemed longer. Certainly the complexities I had struggled with when I first arrived in Cumberland were not over.

Pushing my bewildering memories to the back of my mind, I hoisted my rod, pack and two glistening trout and set off down the Cruikshank River to the lake and my boat. At least there would be fresh fish, sizzling in the pan, for supper.

Fishing was one way that I handled my loneliness in this strange new world. Around the cabin I explored the forest. Instead of being the impenetrable wilderness I had imagined, it was actually crisscrossed by a bewildering network of trails, both human and animal. I found it hard to navigate along them, being used to the openness of the English countryside, but I soon learned my way around. However, there was a much easier way to get about — Uncle Charles' rowboat.

My father had taught me to row and, with free use of the boat, I soon found my way around Comox Lake. I rarely ventured out into the middle, where sudden winds could raise a considerable chop on the water, but there were many miles of coastline awaiting my investigation. Rivers and streams ran into the lake at many places, and these became my thoroughfares where I could go and fish to my heart's content. I could row up the lake, hike into the bush along a river course, fish for a day and still be back in time to cook my catch for supper. I quickly learned to love the woods. I was never lonely there. There was so much going on. The vegetation was a riot of growth, from the smallest flower hidden beside a rotting log, to the tallest Douglas fir soaring far above my head. Through it all there was a bustle of activity as insects, birds, deer and bears went about their business. I could forget how lonely I really was. Best of all, there was no war going on in the woods and I had had enough of any kind of war.

The war in Europe seemed a long way off in Cumberland in the summer of 1918. The casualty lists continued to grow, but America was in now and it would only be a matter of time until the Germans were beaten. Apart from the occasional grieving widow, wounded soldier, and the story of the German mine owner who, rumour had it, had been trying to build submarine pens in the Queen Charlotte

Islands, the war had had little impact on the children of Cumberland, and that was fine by me. But it was changing.

In 1917, the Canadian Government had introduced conscription to force men to go into the army to make up for the horrible casualties of the Somme and Passchendaele. It had not been a popular policy and, for once, mine owners and workers had been united in their hatred of it. You could apply for an exemption from service, and ninety-four percent of the four hundred thousand men called up did, but in the spring of 1918, with the Germans on the offensive in France, all exemptions were suddenly cancelled without explanation. Most men went when they were called, mainly because not to go meant several years in prison doing hard labour, but some went into hiding.

The Cumberland men who refused to go went into the bush around Comox Lake. They lived off the land and people took them food, and the local police didn't try too hard to find them. But then, in June, the government brought in the Dominion Police. Cabins and boats were searched and ambushes were set. Trackers were brought in to hunt the men. What had been a good-natured game of hide and seek, now became much more serious.

My thoughts were interrupted by the sight of the sun-dappled lake, shining blue through the thinning trees. I hauled the boat down to the water, loaded my catch and tackle and pushed off for home.

Saturday, July 20, 1918

EVENING

—᠁—

About two miles down the lake, a powerboat roared out of a small bay and headed toward me. I recognized the big man sitting by the noisy Waterman motor in the stern — Dan Warren, a special constable with the Dominion Police. Warren wasn't a local man, so he stood out, even to a newcomer like me. He had been brought in from Victoria because he was a crack shot with a rifle and an expert hunter. Warren was outwardly cheerful but he was not liked and he had a murky past. Apparently, he had once been a regular provincial policeman in Victoria but had been thrown out of the force for extorting money and threatening witnesses. He had never been reinstated but the government was not above hiring him for special duties such as the work he was doing now.

"Well, well, well, if it ain't young Will Ryan," he said with a slimy smile as the boat drew alongside. "What are you doing out on the lake?"

"Going home."

"And where have you been?"

"Up the lake," I replied, rather enjoying being as curt as possible.

"Now look, lad," he said, the smile fading from his lips. "I am a police officer here on official government business. You wouldn't want word to get back to your uncle that you had been obstructing a constable in the line of duty, would you?"

"No sir," I replied, cowed by the threat of involving Uncle Charles. "I've been fishing on the Cruikshank."

"See anything or anyone unusual?" he went on, his smile returning now that he was back in charge. His eyes bored into me. I felt my face go red and the sweat begin to break out under my collar. I knew I was hesitating suspiciously long.

"No," I blurted out eventually, "no one." Warren stared at me silently for what seemed like an age. I tried to hold his gaze, but I couldn't. I dropped my eyes.

"Any luck?"

"Luck?" I asked, looking up. Warren had his head tilted to one side and was looking at me intently.

"Any luck with the fishing?"

"Oh," I stammered, "a couple of trout is all."

"Let's see them then," he ordered.

Relieved to be doing something and not under interrogation, I lifted the two fish. They were a good size, two- or three-pounders, and their wet scales glistened in the low afternoon sun.

"Nice fish," said Warren, "pass them over."

"What?"

"You heard me," he said, "pass them over. There's food getting up to them boys hid in the woods and I am empowered to confiscate anything suspicious I find in boats on this lake."

"But I'm going down the lake," I protested. "I couldn't be taking food to anyone."

"You're going down the lake now," Warren sneered. "But what's to say you don't turn around and row back up as soon as I am out of sight. Now pass over them fish."

Barely able to control my temper, I hurled the fish over into Warren's boat where they slapped into the pool of water in the bottom.

"Thanks for supper," Warren said, "Now, you head on home sharpish, and think twice before you go wandering around these woods on your own. This ain't Yorkshire and these are dangerous times."

With that he sat back, the engine roared and, in a cloud of spray, the boat swung away.

I sat drifting for some time before I picked up my oars. I was annoyed at losing the fish, but there was something else; I felt guilty that I might have given something away in my hesitation. It was ridiculous, I should have told Warren outright who I had met and where. Even if I didn't like Warren personally, the police were the good guys and the revolutionary Red Goodwin the bad guy. I hadn't planned on hiding the meeting; instinctively it had seemed the right thing to do. My uncle would not be happy if he ever found out.

Thoughtfully, I rowed on down the lake. I had this vague feeling that my denial to Warren was important: that I was being drawn into something I didn't understand.

Supper was not as tasty as it would have been with my trout, but Aunt Sophie had put a nice stew together. Uncle Charles came in and washed up as we sat down to eat.

"Didn't you go fishing today?" he asked as he joined us at the table.

"Yes," I answered quietly, "up on the Cruikshank."

"No luck though?"

"Actually, I caught two nice trout."

My uncle looked up from his plate. "Where are they then, Sophie? This stew is good, but there is little to compare with trout taken fresh from a mountain river."

"Dan Warren took them," I said.

"Dan Warren? The special Dominion Constable?" Uncle Charles asked, turning back to me.

"Yes. I met him on the lake and he confiscated them. Said I might take them up to the draft dodgers hiding in the woods."

A puzzled look crossed my uncle's face. "But you were coming back down the lake, weren't you?"

"Yes, but Warren said I might turn around and row back up."

Uncle Charles paused, frowning. "I agree with what Warren and the others are doing, trying to catch those cowards and revolutionaries, but I think he is getting too big for his boots. I should have a word with Bill Ward and see what he can do."

Ward was the local Provincial Policeman, he was an ex-miner and it was well known that he had sympathies with Goodwin and the others. There was a story told that earlier in the summer he had come upon Goodwin in a cabin in the woods and had shouted and fired his rifle in the air to warn the fugitive and give him plenty of time to escape before he began a search.

Ward had been one of the first to volunteer when the war broke out at the end of the Big Strike and had been Cumberland's first returning war hero. He had been shot through the chest in France. The Italian Band and most of the town came to welcome him back when he stepped off the train in 1915. Whether you agreed with his sympathies or not, everyone knew that Bill Ward was an honest man.

"It's Sunday tomorrow," my uncle continued. "Let's you and me walk into town early and talk to Bill before church. Your aunt can meet us at the church."

"No, it's okay," I stammered, not wanting to become more involved than I already was. "It's only fish."

"It might be only fish to you, Will, but there's a principle here. Just because Dan Warren is a policeman, doesn't mean he is above the law."

I fell silent. There was no point arguing with Uncle Charles once he had made his mind up. He had strong ideas and he stuck to them. But I wasn't happy. I had hoped the fish incident would just disappear.

After supper I went out into the gathering dusk and wandered aimlessly around the forest paths, trying to make sense of my thoughts. Eventually, I found a fallen log and sat down. It was at times like this that my loneliness was worst. My mind drifted back England and all the friends I had had their. There had always been someone at home with whom I could play football or cricket, or explore the countryside, or talk about the war. Here, even though I was prepared to count anyone who talked to me as a friend, I had only two almost friends — Jimmy Wong and Morag McLean.

Even though there were only a few weeks left before summer, one of the first things Uncle Charles did after I arrived was pack me off to Miss Criche's one-room school. He said it was so that I would have a chance to make new friends, but I suspected that it was to get me out of the way. I was beginning to get used to being farmed out and shunted off.

Miss Criche took turns working with each grade while the rest of us were given work to do or left to our own devices. It was not my favourite place, partly because of the strange newness to everything, but mainly because most of the kids were miners' children and they knew I was related to a boss. Despite my best efforts to fit in, it was difficult. Goodwin's war between bosses and workers was very real here. Everyone still remembered the big strike of only four years ago. It had lasted nearly two years and the workers had lost. There had been terrible hardship, families evicted from their homes, workers blacklisted, children starving. Many people had moved away. Those that stayed still remembered the anger and the hardship. Men who had scabbed by working when their comrades were out on strike were still cut dead in the street by their neighbours. There had been riots and violence — and my uncle was one of the hated bosses. Of course, his version was that the miners had become too greedy and needed to be brought down a peg or two, but that must have been a hard theory to stomach for a man watching his family go hungry.

Jimmy, Morag and I were thrown together as the three oldest pupils in the school. After our unpromising beginning, Jimmy and I had become friends, but there were limitations. The Chinese community lived down in the exotic maze of Chinatown where they kept to themselves. They had not supported the big strike and this had added to the bad feeling that some of the men felt about the Chinese coming over and taking their jobs. The fact that the Chinese were poorly paid and were often given the most dangerous work, or that most of the other men had themselves come over or were the children of men who had come over from Italy, Wales, Scotland, or other parts of Europe, did not seem to matter. Even though Jimmy had a white mother, he was still regarded as Chinese, a perception he sometimes encouraged, dressing in traditional clothes on weekends and taking part in Chinese celebrations. I had grown to like Jimmy and we got on well, but neither his family nor mine would tolerate too close a friendship.

My relationship with Morag was different. The gulf between us was equally as wide as the one between Jimmy Wong and me, but Morag seemed less inclined than Jimmy to cross it. Morag tended to keep to herself and there was often a streak of anger in what comments she did make. During the strike, her father had spoken openly in support of better working conditions and the enforcement of the eight-hour working-day law. I think he had avoided blacklisting because he was so obviously interested only in working conditions and made no claims to wanting a violent revolution. He was on the workers' side, but he was a man that the bosses could deal with. That's not to say that he thought kindly of my uncle.

On top of it all, Morag had an older sister, Jenny, who worked in the store in town. It was said that Jenny had a boyfriend — Red Goodwin. Apparently, Goodwin would sneak into town to meet Jenny even though it meant avoiding the likes of Dan Warren.

I tried to stay neutral in the complex war I had been thrust into, but it was not always possible. I had little in common with the workers' children who appeared coarse and ill-educated despite Miss Criche's best efforts. The bosses and other mine managers who came round to talk to Uncle Charles, all appeared much more cultivated and intelligent and I gravitated naturally to their world.

I was abruptly brought back to the present by a sudden noise behind me. Turning, I was surprised to be face-to-face with Morag McLean. I felt the colour rise in my cheeks.

"Hi," I stammered.

"Hello," she replied confidently in her lightly accented voice. Her amazing eyes looked straight at me and her mouth was turned up in a half smile. To my horror, I noticed she was dressed like a man, in loose working pants and a wool shirt. She was carrying a pack slung over her right shoulder. She must have noticed my shocked look.

"Well," she said, "have you ever tried walking through the bush in a long skirt?"

"No, of course not," I replied indignantly.

"Exactly," she said, "you men have the best of everything, even clothes for hiking in the bush. I don't see why women shouldn't do just what men do and why they shouldn't wear the most appropriate clothes to do it in." Morag stood with one leg thrust forward and her left hand on her hip, challenging me to disagree with her.

"Well," I said weakly, "it's not very feminine."

"Hah!" Morag snorted. "Feminine! The government doesn't care too much about femininity when they need someone to work in the munitions factories so they have more men to send to die over in France. I don't see why I should care any more about it when I want to take a walk in the bush."

"Where are you headed?" I asked, desperate to keep the conversation going and yet steer the subject away from this sensitive topic.

Suddenly, Morag seemed less confident. "Oh, just for a walk."

"At night with a pack?" I went on.

"Not that its any of your business," she replied, getting her confidence back, "but I am taking some supplies to Dad's cabin up the lake."

Morag's father's rough, homemade cabin was on the lakeshore near the north end. He, and several other miners, used it as a base for hunting and fishing trips and some men even ran traplines back into the hills. The usual way to get to the cabin was by boat, not a long trek through the woods, especially at night. It didn't make sense — unless you didn't want anyone to see you.

"Okay," I acknowledged, "but it's a long walk at night. And those draft dodgers are about."

"As I told you," Morag said, stepping past me, "it's none of your business."

Morag was several steps away, before I realized something. "Wait! Your cabin is on that small bay about two miles down from the Cruikshank isn't it?"

"Yes," she answered, turning back to face me.

"Well, you probably don't want to go there tonight. I was up that way fishing in the rowboat today and I was stopped and searched by Dan Warren." I could see Morag's body tense as I spoke. "He confiscated my fish and, I think, intended to have them for supper."

"I'm sorry for your loss," Morag interrupted, "but what does this have to do with me?"

"Just this. After Warren took my fish, he was headed back into the bay where your father's cabin is. I think he has a camp there. Maybe he's even squatting in your cabin."

Morag's brow furrowed with worry. "He's no right to use our cabin."

"Come on," I said, deliberately goading her, "anyone can use any cabin they need up in the bush. It's always been that way."

"For friends, yes, but not for scab policemen. Warren's just a bounty hunter. He's been brought in by the bosses for one reason only, and that is to capture Ginger and the others — or worse," she added darkly.

Morag's eyes drifted to focus over my shoulder. She went on, as if to herself. "If Warren stays there tomorrow, then

Ginger might barge into . . ." Abruptly she caught herself and looked back at me.

"So you were taking supplies up to the deserters," I said softly.

"They're not deserters," she said, the fire coming back into her eyes. "The conscription act is criminal, forcing men to go and fight and die in a European war that is none of our concern. And Ginger is too sick to go in any case. He wouldn't last two weeks in the army with his lungs."

I didn't like the war that my father had fought and died in being called none of our concern but, having seen the blood-spotted handkerchief, I couldn't argue with Morag's last point.

"But yes, you guessed right, I am taking supplies," she hesitated, "and I wasn't looking forward to a long, lonely walk in the dark."

Morag looked hard at me. "Can I trust you?"

"Of course. With anything," I said rashly.

"It's just, your uncle is no great friend of the miners or Ginger and the men in the bush. If he were to find out . . ."

"He won't," I interrupted, eager to convince Morag of my trustworthiness. "I went fishing on the Cruikshank this afternoon and met Red Goodwin."

Morag narrowed her eyes and stared at me even more intently. "Where?"

"Up from the river. I heard a voice and went to investigate. He was standing on a tree stump like some old-time preacher, waving his arms about and singing, and trying to convince the surrounding stumps that socialism was the way."

Morag laughed and sat on the other end of my log. It was fairly dark by now, especially in the trees and I could see her only as a dark shape.

"Why didn't you turn him in when Warren stopped you?" she asked.

"I'm not sure. I suppose I should have. He is a criminal, and Uncle Charles will kill me if he ever finds out. But Goodwin didn't seem like the dangerous revolutionary everyone makes him out to be. And he is sick. I saw blood on his handkerchief after he coughed. It just never crossed my mind to turn him in."

I caught a flash of white teeth as a fleeting smile crossed Morag's face in the dusk. But her words were serious when they came. "He's only a danger to those who are out to make a fortune from this war by demanding that men work long hours in unsafe conditions for starvation wages. You saw how sick Ginger is. He was originally classified as Category D — unfit for service. But eleven days after he led the strike in Trail last year, he was called back and reclassified Category A — combat service, overseas."

"That's not fair."

"Of course it's not fair. They wanted to get rid of him. They knew he wouldn't survive a spell in the trenches. If they catch him and send him overseas, it will be murder as clearly as if they shoot him or hang him."

"Come on," I objected strongly, "isn't that a bit much. The government isn't trying to murder anybody."

"Aren't they?" Morag asked. "I like you Will Ryan. You've got a good heart, but you've also got an awful lot to learn about the ways of the world. I suppose it's not your fault that you grew up privileged in England and that your uncle is a boss. Charles Ryan is just trying to do the best he can, but the way to make things better is not for a few men to struggle up to the bosses' level, but to change the system so that there are no more levels at all.

"But there's no time for that now. I need help. Can I really trust you to help and not breathe a word to your uncle or anyone else?"

I was horribly mixed up. On the one hand, I was indignant that this girl was saying I still had a lot to learn. On the other hand, I was flattered that she was asking me for help. Flattery won. Even though I sensed at some level that I was getting in way over my head, I couldn't resist those eyes. In all honesty I would have done anything for Morag had she asked, walked into the lake, even taken on my uncle.

"Of course you can," I said.

"Okay. I was supposed to take these supplies," Morag indicated her pack, "they're mostly sugar, ammunition for hunting, and mail, up to the cabin. It's like a post office in the bush. People leave things there and Ginger comes by and picks them up. He is due to make a pickup tomorrow night."

"Won't he check it out first and see that it's not safe?"

"I don't know," Morag said. "He doesn't treat the hunt seriously enough. He takes too many risks. Just the other night he came right into town to see Jenny. That was stupid. There are police everywhere. I am afraid he might not think and just waltz right into Warren's arms. We have to warn him."

My heart did a somersault at Morag's use of the word *we*. "How?"

"Well, obviously I cannot go up tonight. Even tomorrow would be dangerous to go to the cabin if Warren's still there. But there's another possibility.

"You know the big overhanging rock, a couple of miles up the Cruikshank?"

I nodded.

"Well, that's a post office too. Ginger'll check it on his way down to the cabin tomorrow. If I can leave the supplies and a message warning him about Warren, he won't need to go on. The problem is that I can't walk all that way in broad daylight. I'd have to pass the cabin and the chances of Warren seeing me would be too great. He can't catch me with the supplies or the message."

"So, what can *we* do?" I asked, thrilled at the complex intrigue.

"We can go on another fishing trip tomorrow afternoon. If we row up the lake we might get past Warren without him seeing us. If not, it's easy enough to drop the supplies over the side and write a new note for Ginger. Are you game for it?"

"Yes," I said eagerly.

"Okay. I'll meet you after lunch and we can set off." Morag rose, a dark figure in the twilight.

"The only thing is," I said, thinking that Uncle Charles would not be thrilled if the daughter of a radical socialist, however beautiful, suddenly showed up at the door, "do you know that point with the big eagle tree on it, just north of here?" The figure in front of me nodded. "How about I pick you up there?"

"Okay," she answered, "and not a word," she added in warning as she turned to go back down the trail. Then she stopped. "And thanks."

I sat and watched her disappear into the darkness. Then I threaded my way between the black tree trunks to our cabin. It took me a long time to fall asleep that night. What had I got myself into?

Sunday, July 21, 1918

MORNING

T he morning dawned with the promise of another hot, sunny day. My mind was full of what I had planned with Morag later, but first there was my trip to church with Uncle Charles. We set off early for a brisk two-mile walk into town and found Bill Ward sitting in his dark Sunday suit and tie, on the narrow porch of his home at the other end of Penrith Avenue from Uncle Charles' house.

Ward was of average height and slightly overweight. His hair was dark and receding and he sported a full handlebar mustache. Despite his unremarkable appearance, I and all the other boys in town were in awe of the man. He had been "over there." He had fought in the trenches, perhaps even killed men. Whenever I met him, my eyes always drifted down to his chest, to the spot where a German Mauser bullet had passed completely through. It was partly morbid fascination, partly a sad wish that my own father could sport such a wound.

"Good morning," Ward said cheerily as we approached. "What brings you folks into town so early?"

"Dan Warren," my uncle replied without any preliminaries. "Will here was up the lake fishing yesterday when he was stopped by Warren. On the pretext of preventing food getting to the deserters, Warren stole Will's catch. He even admitted he was going to eat it for supper. Now anyone that knows me knows that no one in my family would ever give any assistance to those men on the run. In fact the opposite. We'd turn them in at the first opportunity."

I winced inwardly at my uncle's misplaced certainty.

"It's a damned disgrace," he went on, "I want something done about it."

Ward looked serious for a moment. Then he said, "Well, Mr. Ryan, I don't think there's anything I can do."

"That's not good enough. You are the law here. You are the authority of the Provincial Government. I know where your sympathies lie and I do not agree with them any more than I daresay you agree with mine. However, this is a clear case of theft, and anyone who steals should have to face the consequences, regardless of their political beliefs."

"I agree," Ward said, "it is a disgrace, and I do not condone it any more than you do. Nevertheless, this is a special case. The Dominion Police are a military force, raised directly by the government and in possession of special powers."

"You mean they are above the law?"

"Not exactly," Ward replied. "If Warren robbed the store or murdered someone, he would go to jail just like anyone else, but it becomes difficult when he can claim that he was carrying out his orders."

"And his orders are to steal fish from children?" my uncle asked angrily.

"No," Ward replied patiently, "but Warren would claim that his orders to prevent food getting to the men on the run allow him enough leeway to confiscate anything he finds on the lake, based only on his own judgment.

"Mr. Ryan, I have seen those orders and they do give Warren and the others a lot of discretion. These are difficult times."

"Difficult times or not, it is still a disgrace."

We were interrupted by two small children, a girl of about seven wearing a checked dress and with her shoulder-length hair tied up by a pale yellow ribbon, and a chubby boy of about five dressed in a sailor suit. They came tearing around the corner of the house, laughing and shouting. They were followed by a thin woman in a dress of the same material as the girl's.

"Peggy, Paul, slow down," the woman was saying, "I don't want those good clothes dirty before church." All three stopped when they saw us.

"Hello, Alice," said Ward standing. "Is it time to go?" The woman nodded. Ward turned back to my uncle, "I'm sorry," he said, "perhaps it would be best if Will stayed off the lake for awhile."

Without a word, Uncle Charles turned and strode down the avenue. "Bye," I said awkwardly as I hurried after him.

We walked in silence along Second Street and down Dunsmuir Avenue, the main thoroughfare in town. Several families were out and about, strolling towards the church. Great effort had been put into grooming grubby children and making threadbare clothes look their best. Uncle Charles nodded curtly at the few people who wished him a "Good Morning."

Aunt Sophie was waiting for us on the church steps dressed in her Sunday best, a checked blue dress whose frills would have marked it as terribly out of date in England but which drew admiring glances here. The church seemed small for the number of people in town, but many of the miners did not attend. I had heard children at school parroting their fathers and saying that religion was just another way of keeping the workers down. I didn't really understand how that could be, but then I also had trouble visualizing God as the old man with a long beard that Sunday School teachers told us about. It was one more complexity that I would eventually have to sort out. For the moment, church on Sunday was simply something to be survived.

As the morning lengthened, and the minister droned on about God being on the side of our brave soldiers in France, and as the temperature in the church rose steadily, heads began to nod and the occasional hymn book thumped from limp hands to the wooden floor. I managed to stay awake, not because the service held my attention, but because I was ignoring it completely. My mind was on the afternoon. It raced through possible scenarios, ranging from romantic picnics with Morag to being caught by Dan Warren and thrown into a rat-infested prison cell. I was no closer to determining which was more likely when we were at last released.

As we gratefully filed out, shook hands with the minister and mumbled something about how good his sermon had been, I noticed Jimmy Wong standing beside the steps, obviously waiting for me.

Because Jimmy's father dressed in western clothes, furnished his house in Chinatown with western furniture, spoke fluent English, and was a Christian, he and his family were allowed to come to "our" church. In exchange for this minor, grudging acceptance by the Europeans, Jimmy's father had to suffer the anger of the traditional Chinese community. He was in charge of the Chinese miners and represented them to the European mine bosses, but that didn't get him much respect. The Europeans resented a "Chinaman" who seemed to them to be getting above himself, and the Chinese miners resented someone who was pandering to the westerners.

Jimmy's mother had the opposite problem. She could never be accepted by the Chinese women, yet she was shunned by the society women who were horrified that she had married outside her race.

Of course, none of this was Jimmy's fault, but he had to live with the consequences. School was sometimes hell for Jimmy. He had to silently bear all kinds of taunts and racist slurs from the bosses' children who regarded the Chinese as little better than work animals, and the workers' sons who often blamed the Chinese for taking jobs away from white miners because they worked for so much less money. It was an impossible situation, but Jimmy bore it with fortitude.

"Hi, Will," he said as I descended the church steps. My uncle and aunt drifted off to talk to someone else.

"Hi, Jimmy," I replied. "It's going to be another hot one."

"Yeah," he said, leading me over to one side, away from the small knots of conversationalists. "I need to talk to you," he said when we were out of earshot.

"What about?"

"About the tunnel to the coal face at the bottom of the deep shaft on Number Four Mine." Jimmy hesitated and I waited, puzzled.

"There's gas collecting there," he went on eventually.

"Then someone should tell the shift foreman," I said.

"Someone did. A group of miners came to see father — they think that, because Mom is white, Dad has influence," Jimmy shrugged eloquently. "Anyway, the miners asked Dad to talk to the shift boss. They said it was too dangerous and the tester needed to go down the shaft."

"Why didn't they go to the shift boss themselves?"

Jimmy looked at me as if I were weak-minded. "If a Chinaman complains," he explained patiently, "he is fired. There are lots more ready to take his job. Why should the shift boss put up with an uppity Chink, when it is so easy to find a quiet one?"

The anger I had heard in Jimmy's words in Vancouver flashed as he used the derogatory, "Chink." I had heard the word used lots of times among both the miners and the bosses. It was so common that it had almost lost its meaning but, coming from Jimmy with his Chinese father, the full hatefulness of the word hit me hard. Maybe that's what Jimmy intended.

"Anyway," Jimmy continued, "Dad went to see the shift boss. He was told that if he didn't shut up he would be fired. He was lucky he wasn't fired on the spot."

My mind created a vivid picture of small, dapper, quiet Mr. Wong, bowing and politely mentioning the possibility of a serious accident if something wasn't done.

"The point is," Jimmy went on, "there is an explosion waiting to happen. Gas is building up and sooner or later the conditions will be right. Dozens of men, white and Chinese, could be killed."

I knew what he meant. I had learned that the coal beneath Vancouver Island was heavily fractured and had a lot of gas in it. If the gas was allowed to collect, it was dangerous. In the right proportion with air, a lethal explosive mixture formed. This could be set off by any spark from a miner's lamp, or from machinery, or blasting at the coal face. Then shock waves and sheets of flame would race through the tunnels and shafts of the mines, faster than a man could run. Miners were crushed, suffocated, and incinerated as they fled. Many people still talked about the tragedy at the Number One Mine in Nanaimo back in 1887. One hundred and forty-seven miners died because a blasting charge had been badly set and ignited gas.

"What can I do?" I asked Jimmy.

"Talk to your uncle. He's the mine manager. He can order a gas test."

I hesitated. Jimmy was right, Uncle Charles had power, but he didn't like the Chinese miners any more than anyone else. I doubted if he would listen to me passing on second-hand information. Testing the tunnels and shafts of Number Four Mine for gas would take time and might mean shutting the mine down for a time. If no coal was being dug, none was being sold, and no money was being made. It was not a decision to be taken lightly.

"Please," Jimmy added, "it's important."

"Will, come on, it's time to go," my uncle shouted from in front of the church where he stood with Aunt Sophie.

"I'll see what I can do," I said as I turned to go.

"Thanks," Jimmy called after me.

"What were you talking with the Wong boy about?" Uncle Charles asked me as the three of us set out for the lake. "You know I am not keen on you spending too much time with him."

"There's nothing wrong with him," I said defensively.

"Oh, he's a nice enough kid. His father has worked very hard to give the boy an education. But it's a waste. He looks too Chinese, and the Chinese have their place in the world. He will never be accepted in white society and it is wrong for his father to let him think that he will. It will only cause grief in the future, you mark my words. All young Wong's hopes will be crushed in time. It would be much easier if he could realize that from the beginning."

I walked in silence for a while, thinking. Uncle Charles was probably right. No one, even the most radical miner, accepted that the Chinese were the same as us or that they could be our equals. The orientals had their place in the world and it was wrong to try and change that. I knew that, but there was a part of me deep inside that was angry: angry that Mr. Wong's determination to improve his family's lot was doomed from the start; angry that Jimmy's hopes would be dashed; and angry that nothing could be done about it.

"They are different from us," Uncle Charles went on. "I'll give you an example. Just yesterday, the boy's father went to the shift boss with some cock-and-bull story about gas building up in the deep shaft. He wanted the mine shut down while we organize a tester. If I did that, we would lose a day's production when prices are the lowest for months and we are struggling just to make a decent profit. The man doesn't even go underground. It's all just the second- or third-hand word of some Chinese labourers who just want a holiday."

"What if there is gas?" I asked quietly, relieved that Uncle Charles had brought the subject up and I didn't have to.

"There's always gas in these mines. If we closed the mine down every time one of the workers complained about something, we would never get anything done. Workers complain. That is their nature. They complain about their wages, their working conditions, the length of their shifts.

"Coal mining is hard work. I'll not deny that, so if the workers, white or Chinese, see a chance to make life easier for themselves they will take it. It's human nature. Ninety-nine times out of a hundred, there is absolutely no basis to the complaints. Next thing you know, Wong'll be coming to me with his frivolous complaints."

"What if the shift boss is wrong? What if this is time number one hundred?"

My uncle stopped walking and looked at me. He was not much taller than I was, but I still had the feeling that he was staring down on me. He had deep-set eyes and they gleamed out from beneath heavy, dark eyebrows.

"What are you getting at?" he asked slowly.

I felt nervous. Uncle Charles had the ability to make me think I had done something wrong just by looking at me.

"It's just that . . . maybe," I stuttered. "Wouldn't an explosion shut the mine down for longer?"

My uncle continued to look at me intently for a long time. Then he turned and resumed walking. I hurried to keep beside him.

"Will," he said eventually, "this is not number one hundred. I cannot shut down production and cost the company thousands of dollars. You are new here. You don't understand all the different factors that come into play in running something as big as a coal mine. Something like an unnecessary test can throw the whole schedule off. In time you will see that I am right."

"But —"

"No buts," Uncle Charles interrupted me firmly. "This conversation is over."

We walked in silence for awhile. There was nothing I could do. I just had to hope that Uncle Charles was right.

But something else was bothering me. Bill Ward had recommended I stay off the lake. How seriously was my uncle taking that? I had to be careful. The one thing I had going for me was the fact that Uncle Charles loved fresh fish.

"There's a big trout in that fishing hole I was at yesterday," I said.

"Really, did you see him?"

"Yes, just a glimpse, but he's hiding in the shade under an overhang. The time to get him would be late afternoon when the insects start flying again and he comes out to feed."

Uncle Charles hummed to himself thoughtfully. "Perhaps we could go up and try our luck this afternoon."

I panicked. That would be even worse than forbidding me to go on the lake. What could I say?

Fortunately, Aunt Sophie came to the rescue. "Not this

afternoon, Charles. You have to fix the porch step and you've got that meeting at the mine this evening."

"Damn. So I do."

I saw my chance. "I'll go and get him for us. We'll cook him up with some butter after you get back from the meeting."

"All right," Uncle Charles laughed. "You go and get him, but be careful you don't run into Dan Warren." Then he turned more serious. "And be sure that if you see anything suspicious, you head back right away. There's strange things going on these days."

"Sure," I said happily. At least one hurdle had been jumped.

Sunday, July 21, 1918

AFTERNOON

—⁓—

A light breeze ruffled the water of the lake and made the work of rowing almost bearable in the heat. Morag had been waiting as planned beneath the eagle tree and now she sat, her pack at her feet, in the stern of the boat. She had changed out of the pants of the night before and wore a long, plain skirt. Her work shirt was replaced by a red cotton blouse. My fishing rod and tackle lay in the bottom of the boat.

"So you managed to escape your uncle?" Morag asked, smiling.

"He wanted to come with me," I said, and the smile vanished.

"How'd you stop him?"

"I didn't have to. Aunt Sophie reminded him he had to fix the porch steps, and he has a meeting at the mine."

"Lucky for us the bosses have plenty of time to go to meetings," Morag said, the smile returning. "I don't know what'd happen if they ever had to do any real work."

"My uncle works hard," I said indignantly, stung by Morag's insult, "and he has a lot of responsibility."

"Okay," Morag conceded, "I'm sure he works long hours and has a lot of worries, but it's not the same as twelve hours bent double at the coal face breathing so much coal and rock dust that your lungs rot." Morag's voice rose as she warmed to her topic, "I've seen men who cough up blood and are so weak their wives have to help them walk out to the outhouse. They'd be happy to have the responsibility of a well-paid office job."

Fire glistened in Morag's eyes as she spoke. I was torn apart. She was ripping into what I said and viciously criticizing my uncle — but she was so beautiful.

"Don't exaggerate," I said defensively. "I know mine work is hard, but nobody works twelve-hour shifts, it's against the law."

Morag laughed. "Sure, it's against the law, but who enforces the law?"

"The police."

"And who pays the police?"

"The government."

"And do you see any workers in the government?"

"No," I had to admit.

"Exactly! The government is made up of men from the same class as the coal bosses. They have the same background, the same outlook and the same interests. Until you see workers in the government — or women for that matter — you won't see any change."

"Women in the government. Women don't even have the vote."

"That may be true in England, but women have the vote in Alberta, Saskatchewan and Manitoba. And it'll happen here. You can't keep half the population without the vote forever."

"But women aren't interested in politics."

Morag laughed so hard she almost tipped the boat. "Will Ryan, you have a lot of growing up to do.

"But we're getting away from what we were talking about. There is a law that says a man can only work an eight-hour day. But, imagine this — your uncle says to a man, you have to work longer, nine, ten, twelve hours. What can the man do?"

"Refuse."

"Okay, so he refuses. Your uncle says, you're fired. What then?"

"The worker goes to the government."

"Easier said than done. I don't think there is anyone to go to, but let's assume there is. The worker goes to the government and says that he was fired because the company tried to make him work more than the legal limit. Assuming again, and this is a big assumption, that he is not just thrown out of whatever office he has found, the government goes to your uncle and asks what happened. Your uncle says that of course the company obeys the laws, but sometimes men have to work overtime, there's a war on. The government wouldn't want production to slacken off and put the brave fighting men at risk. Besides, this man is a known trouble-maker. He can't be trusted.

"The government says fine, and the worker's left in the lurch. He has no job and the company'll blacklist him. He'll never be able to get a job again. How's his family going to eat?"

Morag tilted her head and looked quizzically at me. I felt flustered and confused. Were things really that bad? I concentrated on rowing for awhile.

"It's not fair," I said at last.

"No, it's not," Morag agreed, "but that's the way it is. The company has all the power, and their only concern is how to make a bigger profit. Profit is their reason for existing in the first place. Look at your own country. The coal companies used to put children to work down the mines."

"But they don't any more."

"No, and why not?"

"Because it's wrong," I ventured.

"It is wrong," Morag said, "but it was just as wrong a

hundred years ago when they were quite happy to do it.

"My great grandfather was a child labourer in Scotland. Father remembers him as an old man, bent over from all the years at the coalface. He had been particularly prized because he was a small child and could work thin seams that adults couldn't get to. Even then, there were laws limiting the hours children could work underground, but nobody paid any attention. Children were too profitable. It was only when technology advanced enough to make child labour underground unprofitable that it was possible to make it illegal. If it were still profitable today, there would still be children like my great grandfather down the mines."

I rowed on in silence. I didn't know what to say. Here was this beautiful girl sitting in the boat talking about children, her ancestors, working down coal mines — and seeming to know more about it than I had been taught in history class at school. It was bizarre.

The silence stretched on as we approached the bay where Dan Warren had stopped me the day before. We both kept glancing nervously over at the shore but no boat came out to intercept us. Either Warren was not paying attention or he was off somewhere else chasing shadows. Gradually we both relaxed as we neared the Cruikshank River.

"So far so good," I said as we pulled the boat up onto the gravel shore.

"Yes," Morag agreed, lifting her pack onto her back. "That was the dangerous bit."

I hoisted the tackle box and my fishing rod out of the boat and we set off along the river bank. It was a beautiful afternoon. The sunlight sparkled off the water burbling over the rocks in the river bed. Sometimes the river bank was clear, but mostly we followed rough trails or waded through the shallows. Occasionally, the curving bed of the river opened to provide views of the mountainous spine of Vancouver Island where puffy clouds clung to the peaks. Perhaps this wasn't such a bad part of the world after all. Of course walking with Morag helped.

"It's a beautiful day," I said in a lame attempt to open conversation.

"Yes," Morag answered smiling. "Are you starting to appreciate our wild part of the world?"

"It's very different from home."

"Tell me about home."

"It's not really home any more," I said. "I suppose this is my home now."

"But you still miss England. Tell me about it."

"Yes, I do miss it. This place is beautiful, but it is wild. If we were to turn and walk into the trees, in minutes we would be completely lost in a wilderness that has never felt a human footfall. In England you are never far away from someone else and the whole country has been tamed. Around the next corner, over the next hill, through the next hedgerow, is a village that has been there for centuries. Families have lived in the same town since before Henry the

Eighth married his first wife. Here everyone is new."

"What about the Indians?" Morag pointed out. "They have been here for thousands of years."

"Yes, but they don't try to alter things. The settlers try to change things but I think it's impossible. Even the big towns, like Vancouver, seem to be clinging to the edge of the wilderness. If the people left, the forest would take over again in a very short time. We haven't made any significant change. In England . . ."

"Oh, ain't that sweet." The hulking figure of Dan Warren stood, blocking the path ahead of us. He held a 30-30 hunting rifle across his chest. I had been so wrapped up in my talk that I hadn't even noticed him step out of the trees. Morag had dropped behind me.

"Two love birds out for a stroll," Warren sneered. "I sure enjoyed those fish last evening, Will Ryan, thank you kindly."

"My uncle has put in a complaint about you stealing those fish," I said, stretching the truth a bit. It had no effect on Warren.

"Is that so," he said. "I'm frightened. Who did he complain to? That namby-pamby friend of the deserters, Bill Ward? I reckon that German bullet must have hit Ward in the head. He doesn't seem to know which side he's on. If I was to come upon that Red Goodwin there would be no shooting harmlessly in the air. I don't miss."

"You're here to arrest people, not kill them," Morag's voice came strongly from beside me.

"Oh, that's right." The sneer was back in Warren's voice. "So I am. I hope that, when I do meet him, I am not so frightened of the big bad Red Goodwin that I miss my aim and kill him by mistake. That would be such a shame.

"So, you kids are off on a fishing expedition, are you? Or perhaps," Warren leered at Morag, "the fishing rod's just for show and you're off into the woods for a bit of fun. I must say I admire your choice, young Ryan."

I felt my cheeks flush red. Before I could think of a reply, Warren continued.

"I'll take a look in that tackle box," he said, "and that pack, young lady."

I tensed. Because out on the lake was where Warren had stopped me yesterday, I had thought the dangerous bit of the journey had been there but it wasn't. If he had tried to catch us there, we would have had plenty of warning to drop the sack with its incriminating supplies over the side of the boat. Here on the trail, we were trapped.

"You have no right," I blustered.

"I have every right," Warren interrupted. "Now pass over those bags before I forget my manners and whip some respect into you two."

Meekly, I placed the tackle box on the ground in front of me and opened the lid. Morag placed her pack beside it. I tried to catch her eye, but she fixed her gaze on the ground in front. What would Warren do when he found the supplies and the ammunition? Already he had dismissed my tackle box and was fiddling with the straps on Morag's pack. Wild ideas rushed through my brain. Warren had placed his rifle on the ground. I could grab it and threaten him. Tell him to leave the bag alone. Then what? It would be an admission of guilt, just as damning as the supplies. I could hardly kill Warren.

"All right then," Warren had straightened up. He sounded disappointed. "You're lucky this time. Off you go and catch some fish. Perhaps I'll see you on the way back. I certainly did enjoy those fish yesterday."

Picking up his rifle, Warren stepped aside and watched us lift our gear and continue up the trail. My mind was a turmoil. Why had he let us go? As soon as we were safely out of sight and earshot, I turned to Morag. She was smiling.

"I didn't bring the supplies, Will," she said. "I cached them in a sack by the eagle tree. If Warren was as suspicious as you said he was, then this is just the sort of trick he might pull. The important thing is to get a message to Ginger. We couldn't do that if Warren caught us with groceries. The supplies can wait for another day."

Morag's smile broadened. "You looked so worried back there."

"I was," I said. "That man scares me."

Morag's smile faded. "He scares me too. All that talk about shooting and not missing. He doesn't sound as if he is out to arrest anyone."

"No," I said thoughtfully. "Will Warren catch Goodwin and the others, do you think?"

"Not unless someone betrays them, and that's not likely. It's wild country up on Alone Mountain where everyone thinks the men are hiding. The constables mostly stay north of the Cruikshank and the creeks that run into it. They hope to catch the men travelling."

"Where everyone *thinks* the men are hiding?"

Morag stared hard at me. "I *can* trust you, Will Ryan, can't I?"

"Of course you can. I will never breathe a word of this to anyone."

Morag continued to stare. Then she shrugged as if coming to a decision. "I don't believe you would.

"The constables have it all wrong. The men are camped south of the Cruikshank. It's even rougher country in there and the hunting's poorer, so it means they have to come over to the Cruikshank to fish and they must rely on supplies from the town more than they would like, but it fools idiots like Dan Warren who always just look for the obvious answer to a problem. As long as no one talks, and as long as Ginger is careful, they should be able to last out the war."

With that thought in our heads, we walked up the river in silence.

Sunday, July 21, 1918

EVENING

—⁓—

I t took Morag and me a long time to work our way up the river. Despite the urgency of our mission, we didn't hurry, stopping often to cast a fishing line in the water and sit by the river bank, just in case Warren had decided to try and follow us. We saw no sign of pursuit, but my half-hearted attempts at fishing produced no results either. My uncle was not going to have trout for supper this evening.

The rock sat by the river bank where it had come to rest years before after its violent journey down the mountain-side. It was the size of a small house and a dark, reddish brown, its surface rough, fractured, and spotted with circles of grey lichen. The only exception was the face closest to the river, which was smooth, almost polished. Twelve thousand years before, high on the valley wall, this face must have been uppermost, polished by the inexorable movement of thousands of feet of ice flowing from the mountains.

By the time we arrived, the puffy clouds I had seen earlier over the mountains had grown to become a large, rolling, grey presence that loomed over us and darkened the bright summer evening. The air had become heavy and oppressive, confirming my suspicion that there were thunderstorms in the offing. Morag worked quickly and silently. She took a sheet of paper and a stubby pencil from a side pocket of her pack and scrawled a quick warning to Goodwin:

"Cops at cabin. Don't go. Will leave supplies here at first chance. A friend."

The abrupt tone and the enigmatic signature gave the whole affair an air of mystery. I found myself looking around nervously.

When she was done, Morag folded the paper and placed it carefully under a flat stone, hidden by the big rock's overhang. Anyone glancing casually as they passed by would see nothing unusual. You would have to know where to look to recover the note.

"There," Morag said with satisfaction as she stood up. "Ginger will find that when he checks here on his way to the cabin." She paused and glanced up at the threatening sky. "We had better hurry if we don't want to be caught on the lake in the storm that's coming." Morag swung her pack over her shoulder and headed off back down the trail. Grabbing my rod and tackle box, I hurried after her.

Now that we had placed the warning, I began to have doubts. It had all seemed like a big adventure this morning — a prank spiced by Morag's presence. But I was no longer so sure. What exactly had I done? I had helped a deserter, a nice-enough person but a criminal despite that, to escape justice. It meant nothing that the criminal was a more likeable person than the policeman who was chasing him — that didn't affect the seriousness of his crime. And most difficult of all, what would my father have thought? He had never talked much about the war, but what he had said had always been positive.

"We have to fight. I didn't want this war to come, but it has and there is no point in sitting around moaning about it. We live in a world that is at war and I can see no way that I can help stop it without one side or the other winning. So I fight for my country and because I believe the Germans are more to blame for starting the war than anyone else and I do not want to see them dominate Europe. We make choices and take sides in a world we cannot control. It is not easy, but I will take my turn."

Goodwin wasn't taking his turn. What's more, he was fighting against the war effort by leading strikes and stirring up trouble. What if his rabble-rousing speeches did have an effect on the supply of either men or material to the soldiers who were fighting? Maybe someone would die, someone like my father, because a shell was not there to destroy a

German machine gun nest or because the reinforcements were not there to press home an attack. I suddenly felt like a traitor. How could I explain to a boy my age that I was helping someone who might be responsible for his father's death in the trenches?

I was deep in thought as I caught up with Morag, so her stark question took me by surprise. "How did your father die?"

"He was buried alive," I said tentatively. I had never talked to anyone about Father's death.

The path was wider here and Morag was walking beside me. She smiled encouragement. I could deny her nothing, even though dredging up the memories was painful. "I remember the last time I saw him. It was June a year ago. I was living with my grandparents. It was incredibly boring and I spent a lot of time sitting in the window alcove daydreaming and looking out over their driveway to the stream that ran down to the old mill.

"I knew he was coming home, but I didn't know exactly when. I expected a phone call from London to say what train he would be on, so I didn't immediately recognize the dapper, uniformed figure that turned into the drive from the road. Dad was a Captain in the King's Own Yorkshire Light Infantry and he looked tremendous in his uniform. He used to let me try it on sometimes. Of course, it was much too big and I looked ridiculous but I loved the rough feel of the cloth and the weight of the leather belt.

"Anyway, he had taken about six steps before I recognized

him. I doubt if he took another six before I had charged out of the room, bolted through the front door, raced down the path and flung myself into his arms."

I paused as I remembered that time. Morag waited patiently.

"The two weeks that followed were the best of my life. I think Dad found my grandparents as boring as I did and we spent almost the whole time together. We walked, played in the gardens, went fishing and talked. He never talked of the war, but we covered every other subject under the sun. I was the luckiest boy in the world. But then he had to go back to his unit."

I felt tears pool in the corners of my eyes. I cleared my throat and forced them back.

"Two months later, the day after my sixteenth birthday, I sat in the same window watching a policeman come up the drive with a telegram saying my father had been killed in action."

I breathed deeply to keep myself under control. Morag placed a sympathetic hand on my shoulder.

"A letter came too, a few days later. It was from one of father's fellow officers. It said how much he would be missed and what a good officer he had been. He was killed when a tunnel collapsed on top of him."

"He was a miner?"

"No, but some men in his company were. They were digging a tunnel to place explosives beneath the German trenches before an attack that was coming up. Both sides tried to do that all the time.

"Anyway, the German miners must have heard the men working and broke into the tunnel. A fight started and my father went down to help. Most of the miners got out, but the Germans set grenades and the roof caved in and buried my father. They never recovered his body."

I wiped the tears from my cheeks. Morag squeezed my shoulder.

"The weeks after the telegram and letter are a blur. In fact, I can barely remember anything of that whole winter. I moped around, getting in everybody's way. I must have been a terrible trial for my grandparents. I just couldn't get any enthusiasm up for anything. What was the point now that father was dead?

"Maybe if I had not been so difficult then, grandfather wouldn't have sent me to live with Uncle Charles."

We walked on in silence for a time, each locked in private thoughts. Then a cold, wet, raindrop splashed against my cheek. I looked up. Large drops were plummeting down through the trees. The clouds were black and heavy. The first rumbles of thunder began echoing down the valley. Morag glanced at the sky and picked up her pace. We were almost running over the rough trail, the tackle box banging uncomfortably against my hip.

The heavy raindrops were rustling the trees around us and patterning the river's surface. I was getting wet. Not that

that was a particular concern; what was more worrying was the wind that was swirling through the treetops. On a long narrow lake like Comox, a squally wind bursting down from the mountains could cause a horrible confusion of choppy waves that could swamp a small rowboat. And there was another danger. Flashes of lightning, immediately followed by rolling clashes of thunder, lit up the trees in an almost unearthly white glow. Out on the flat lake, the rowboat would stand out and be a magnet for a lightning strike. The voyage down the lake was becoming more dangerous by the minute. Then I tripped.

Perhaps I wasn't paying attention, perhaps it was inevitable given the wet, slippery roots sticking up all over the path. In any case, I slipped on a root and tumbled sideways. My left foot turned under me and a bolt of pain seared through my ankle. I cried out as I landed heavily on my side. In a moment, Morag was crouching over me, a look of concern on her face.

"Are you all right?" she asked.

"Yes," I replied bravely but untruthfully. Just how untruthfully was revealed the moment I tried to put any weight on my twisted ankle. In a wash of pain it gave way and I fell back onto the ground.

"Here, let me help." Morag draped my left arm across her shoulder and took as much of my weight as she could. Putting all the rest of my weight on my good ankle, I managed to stand. Walking was another matter and running at our previous speed out of the question. Awkwardly on the narrow path and with many halts for breath, we staggered along. Around us the storm intensified. The thunder and lightning were simultaneous now, deafening and blinding. The rain came down in torrents and we were already both soaked through. I couldn't see how we could make it down the lake under these conditions. It would be madness. We were looking at a night in the open under very unpleasant circumstances.

Oddly, I was happy. Unreasonably and stupidly, but I couldn't help it. My arm was around Morag's shoulder and with every awkward, halting step, I could feel her close beside me. That was all that mattered. Whatever happened, it would happen while we were together. If I hadn't been grimacing in pain with every step, I would have been smiling.

I was beginning to wonder if we would even reach the boat, when Red Goodwin stepped out onto the path ahead of us. For a horrible moment, I thought it was Warren come back to taunt us in our misery, but the red hair, even plastered down by the rain, was a giveaway. He looked incongruous in his suit in the middle of the storm in the wilderness.

"Nice day for a walk," he shouted cheerfully above the noise of the downpour. "You look as if you might need a hand."

"What are you doing here?" Morag shouted at the soggy figure in front of us.

"Going for a Sunday afternoon stroll," Goodwin replied stepping forward. "As far as I am aware, the forests of British Columbia are still open and free for the use of every man." Then he added with a wink at me, "Not like the estates of the landed aristocracy in the old country, eh?

"Where are you headed?"

Morag ignored his question. "Where are *you* going?"

"Why, the weather is so fine, I thought I might wander down to pick up the supplies a little early, then maybe stroll into town to visit my girl."

"Are you going to visit the overhanging rock?" Morag asked.

A puzzled expression crossed Goodwin's face. "Hadn't planned on it. I thought I'd just take the direct route down the lake shore."

"You're a fool, Ginger Goodwin." Morag's voice was strong and hard.

Goodwin frowned. "Now . . ."

But Morag didn't give him a chance. "You don't take this seriously and it will cost you. What's the point in having a system if you ignore it? We have just come all the way up the lake to leave a warning, and you don't even check it out."

"A warning?" Goodwin tried to interrupt, but Morag was in full flight and wouldn't let him.

"Yes, a warning. Warren and his cronies are all over these woods. Will was stopped by him yesterday and says he is staying at my father's cabin on the bay."

Goodwin glanced over at me.

"And he stopped and searched us on the way upstream this afternoon," Morag continued. "You would just have waltzed into the cabin without a care in the world, straight into the arms of the Dominion Police. When are you going to realize that this is not a childish game of hide-and-go-seek? Warren is armed and dangerous. You must take this seriously."

Goodwin relaxed and smiled. "Lucky I ran into you then." Morag groaned in frustration, but Goodwin continued. "Speaking of fools. I don't suppose you two serious revolutionaries were contemplating trying to make it back down the lake in this weather? I estimate that you would last about ten minutes before a wave swamped your boat or a bolt of lightning fried you." As if to emphasize his words, a particularly bright flash of lightning lit us up and a crash of thunder shook the ground beneath our feet.

"We could walk around the lake," Morag said defiantly.

"Yes, you could," Goodwin acknowledged, "but that would only prolong the agony as you slowly died of pneumonia. I was even thinking of turning back myself and you know what a reckless fool I can be."

Goodwin waited in silence for a moment, but Morag said nothing, so he went on.

"I have a suggestion. Warren is going to be well set up, warm and dry in your father's cabin. The weather is not going to improve before dark. It looks to me as if you are stuck up here for the night. Now, I have a small camp set up over the first ridge. I even have a stash of dry firewood. My suggestion is that we head over there and, as soon as this storm abates, get a fire going and dry things out a bit. It's not the Empress Hotel, but then I don't see that you have much choice. This way you won't be dead of drowning, electrocution, or pneumonia."

Morag looked thoughtful. I was doubtful. I didn't want to be in debt to this man, but what he said made sense. And the pain in my ankle was getting worse. What alternative did we have?

"All right," Morag said at last.

"Good," said Goodwin cheerfully. Over Morag's protests, he stepped in and took the weight off my injured leg. Oddly, although Goodwin was bigger than Morag, he felt almost fragile. Instinctively, I took as much of my weight on my sore ankle as I could. Turning away from the river, stumbling through the trees, and panting our way uphill, we set off.

Sunday, July 21, 1918

NIGHT

—᭘᭘᭘—

T he journey up to the ridge was a nightmare. The track was much more tortuous than the one along the river, in places only a deer trail, and it was often not wide enough to permit anyone to help me. Over these stretches I had to drag myself up by tree branches or crawl on my hands and knees. Around us the lightning flashed in blinding bursts and the thunder deafened us. My ankle felt as if it were on fire, and Goodwin, even when he wasn't helping me, had to stop frequently to catch his breath and, more than once, gave in to wracking fits of coughing.

By the time we had struggled to the top of the ridge, all three of us were exhausted and darkness was falling, but at least the rain had eased and the storm was moving away. My lungs felt as if they were on fire and I was covered in scratches and bruises. Lightning still lit up the landscape and illuminated the wind-whipped whitecaps on the lake, but it was playing around the mass of clouds in the distance and there was a gap of several seconds between the flashes and the thunder. I was really glad I was not out on the water in an open boat.

"Not far now," Goodwin gasped as we started on the down slope.

Fortunately, he was right and we were soon collapsing in pitiful, soaking heaps in a small clearing. There was a blackened fire pit in the middle. The rain had tailed off to a drizzle that would have been annoying had we not already been completely soaked. After a moment or two, Goodwin dragged himself to his feet. "Better get a fire going before it gets too dark. I hope my kindling stayed dry."

Picking up a flat piece of wood, Goodwin scraped the wet ash out of the fire pit. Then he stumbled to the edge of the clearing and dragged a large canvas sack out from under a clump of ferns.

"I can't offer you much in the way of supper," he said, "but maybe we can warm up a bit." It was only then that I noticed that my teeth were chattering from the cold.

From his bag, Goodwin produced a clump of dry twigs and moss, and some small split sticks. These he arranged in the fire pit and carefully placed some larger sticks on top.

Working quickly so that the kindling didn't have a chance to get wet, he took out a box of sulphur matches and lit the pile. As the crackling flames grew, Goodwin added larger pieces of wood until we had a good fire going. Then he sat back. Morag and I shuffled closer. The warmth felt good and already my clothes were beginning to steam.

"This is just a way-station," Goodwin told me, "a transit camp near our favourite fishing hole or on the way down the lake. Our main camp is farther south, up by Cougar Lake. It's rough country and it means we have to walk cross-country some way to do any decent fishing on the Cruik-shank, but so far no one has thought to look for us up there. That's where Arthur, Fred and Jimmy are right now. We only use this if we get back too late from fishing or a trip down the lake. You don't want to be wandering around this country in the dark."

In the flickering light from the fire, my mind conjured vivid images of sleek, hungry cougars prowling the wooded shores of a mountain lake while bears growled in the background. It was all I had imagined the Canadian wilderness to be.

"How's your ankle?" Goodwin asked.

"Not too bad," I said. "Thanks for helping me up the hill."

Goodwin shrugged. "We all have to help each other, right?"

Morag and I nodded.

Goodwin looked at Morag. "So you came all the way up

here, braving the weather and Dan Warren, to warn me not to go to the cabin?

"Well, I thank you." Goodwin turned back to me. "And you, young Will Ryan. Did you come to warn me or was there an ulterior motive?" I felt myself blush despite the cold, but Goodwin went on before I was too embarrassed.

"What would Charles Ryan say if he could see his nephew sitting around a fire with a dangerous revolutionary?"

"He wouldn't be happy," I said.

"That's an understatement. I should think he would be furious. After all, I am the man who is winning the war for the Germans."

All the anger I felt at Goodwin's betrayal of my father and all the other brave soldiers, suddenly swept over me.

"Maybe he would be angry, but it's none of your business." Goodwin shrugged and held up his hands to placate me, but I wouldn't have any of it. I was incensed at the complexity this man had introduced into my life. It was difficult enough trying to fit into this new life in this wild new world, without having someone like Goodwin criticize my family.

"You all seem to think my uncle is so bad. He's not. He's just an ordinary man trying to do the best he can and make something of his life. Can you blame him for that? He's not evil."

"No, I daresay he's not," Goodwin said. "He's just as much a slave — a pawn in the real bosses' game — as the miner working the coal face. I can't respect him because he does what he does for money and social position, but I don't think he is evil. The real evil men are the owners in Victoria and Ottawa. They have the money and influence to change the world, to make it a better place for ordinary working people, but they don't. Instead they use all their power to make more money and to line their own nests — nests that are soaked with the blood of honest men — soldiers as much as miners."

"That's melodramatic. The owners aren't monsters. They care."

Goodwin looked thoughtfully at me for a moment. "I'll tell you a story. Back at Christmas 1901, when James Dunsmuir still owned all the mines hereabouts, the miners down at the Extension Mine in Nanaimo had to travel to Ladysmith to collect their wages. It was twelve miles by train but they had to wait eight hours for the return journey. It cost them a full day every payday.

"The union formed a committee to ask Dunsmuir if the miners could be paid at Extension. A reasonable request that would cost Dunsmuir nothing and was made during the season of goodwill. Do you know what Dunsmuir's response was?"

I shook my head.

"Dunsmuir said, 'To hell with the union, to hell with the committee, to hell with the men.' Does that sound like someone who cares?"

"No," I said, shocked at Dunsmuir's callousness. "But Uncle Charles cares."

"So, why isn't he testing for gas in the mine?" Morag

joined in angrily. "That sounds like someone who will let men die rather than lose production of his precious coal."

"That's not fair," I shot back.

"Fair isn't part of it." Morag's eyes gleamed in the firelight. "Your uncle doesn't care about having blood on his hands. He's a puppet of the owners and that makes him just as bad. He's . . ."

"Wait!" Goodwin's command silenced Morag. As we both stared at him, his face broke into a smile, drawing the tension out of the air. "You two behave like an old married couple. Here we are, three more-or-less reasonable people sitting in the middle of nowhere, and all we can do is argue. If we can't be civilized here, what hope is there?

"I don't know Charles Ryan. Perhaps he doesn't care. Perhaps he lies awake nights agonizing over gas in the mine. Either way, he has no choice. The company sets the rules and enforces them. The company pressures Ryan and the other managers to meet production quotas and keep profits up. No one could go against that and expect to keep their job long. The problem is not individuals; it's the system. As long as profit for the few at the top is the motivation, no one will care about those at the bottom."

I struggled with the idea that people were trapped by the circumstances of their birth. My father had always taught me that the individual could do whatever he really put his mind to, but then, I suppose he was looking at it from a privileged position where he had choices. I didn't have long to dwell on it, Goodwin was in full flight.

"It's the same with the war. The motivations of those at the top, regardless of which country they belong to, have nothing to do with what motivates the average soldier to fight and die. The men in power want markets and empires. The soldiers are being fooled into believing they are fighting for King and Country. In reality, they have more in common with the soldiers on the other side of no-man's-land than they do with their own officers. A bayonet has been described as a weapon with a worker at both ends."

"My father believed in what he fought for." Mention of the war refocused my anger. "He was a good man who died in the war that you spend so much energy trying to avoid. The war may not be a good thing, but it has to be fought. Germany has to be stopped from taking over Europe. Thousands of men are dying to do that. Maybe you are sick and cannot fight, but there is still lots that you could do, working in a hospital or a factory or something; instead of skulking in the woods like an animal. But that's not the worst. The strikes you lead can stop vital material getting to the war effort. Men are dying because of what you do and that is criminal. Much worse than your own personal cowardice."

I stopped, as surprised as the other two by my outburst. Morag looked shocked and Goodwin looked thoughtful. As the silence dragged out, I became more and more embarrassed. It was Morag who broke it at last.

"That's not fair. Ginger's not hurting anyone with his convictions. He's just . . ."

"No." Goodwin spoke softly, but it was enough to stop

Morag and hold both our attention. "Will is right. Men do die because of what I do. I know that, and I lie awake at night thinking on it."

"Then why go on doing it?" I interrupted.

"Because I chose a side. Not a side within the war, but one against the war. I saw no other way.

"You think of the war in terms of individuals fighting one another. That is natural enough, it is what the newspapers tell us all the time, but it is not true. This war has a life of its own and individuals — men, women and children — who are caught up in its horror are only the fuel that keeps it going. Think of the war as a machine — a huge meat-grinding machine. All the countries of the world, Britain, Germany, France, Austria, Turkey, Italy, Japan, Canada, and now America, are a part of that machine. They are the wheels and cogs that run it. Their job is to provide the fuel for the war, collect men from everywhere, even these remote valleys on Vancouver Island, and feed them into the war. And it is endless, because the more men that are fed into the war, the more men it wants.

"When I speak out against the war, I am not speaking against brave men like your father. I am speaking against the war itself, against the machine that killed him, and will go on killing millions of others until someone has no fuel left for the war, or until what fuel is left says enough.

"The Russians have already said enough. Others will before this is over."

"Britain will never stop fighting," I said patriotically.

"She may not have a choice. What has happened in Russia is spreading. The French armies mutinied last year. Thousands refused to fight and, on their way to the front lines, entire regiments bleated like sheep being led to the slaughter. Their officers had to shoot dozens of their own men to force the others to return to the trenches. There are signs of unrest in Germany. Even British troops, so famous for doing what they are told, mutinied at the base at Etaples last year."

"I don't believe you," I shouted.

"But it's true. For several days, the soldiers took over the base and the local town and refused to work or fight. Military policemen, hated at the best of times, were hunted down and killed. The base commander was a virtual prisoner in his own quarters.

"Now, I admit that this is a small incident and not likely to bring down the government, but it is a start. And it is certainly a change from the cheerful enthusiasm of 1914.

"It is only through encouraging these small rebellions to grow and become revolutions, that we can destroy the machine that is the war and prevent the same thing happening again and again and again."

"But why should it happen again?" I asked.

"It's inevitable," Goodwin replied, "because that is the way things are set up. All the developed countries are in competition for markets. Britain is so successful because she has an empire, places like Canada and India where she can get raw material and where she can sell manufactured goods.

"Think about it. Who buys the coal your uncle organizes the miners to dig out from beneath our feet? Who makes the dresses your aunt wears and the cutlery and crockery in her kitchen? The answer to both questions is Britain. It's a cycle of business that brings vast profits to those in power. Germany wanted some of those profits and Britain didn't want to give her any. That is why they became competitive and, eventually went to war — over markets. Oh, the circumstances might change, the next war might be over something like this new fuel, oil, but the root cause is the same — competition in business leads to competition on the battlefield. The only way to stop it is to get rid of the competition in business, as they have done in Russia. Then there will be no more war and men like your father won't have to go and die so that someone who stays at home remains rich."

"That's not right," I said, confusion whirling around my head. "The world's not that complicated. Germany tried to invade France through neutral Belgium and Britain went to war to help Belgium. It's as simple as that."

"Is it?" Goodwin asked.

"Yes," I said a little too loudly. "It's not a huge conspiracy of businessmen."

"No," Goodwin said, "it's not a conspiracy, but that doesn't mean the war wasn't inevitable. Why did Germany invade France? Her people were happy. They had plenty of food and land. Why did Germany try to build more battleships than Britain? She's not an island, in fact she is almost land-locked. Germany doesn't need a huge navy. There has to be a reason for a country to go to war. Somebody with power, a king, or an emperor, or all the rich businessmen, must feel that they will gain something valuable enough to make all the disruption of war worthwhile. What was it in 1914?

"The answer is an empire. Germany wanted to defeat France and Britain so that she could take colonies away from them both. Then she would have an empire just like Britain, and all her factories would have lots of raw materials to make things with and lots of markets to sell things to."

I sat in silence trying to absorb what Goodwin was say-ing. Instinctively, I wanted to reject his ideas. I had grown up with the simple version of the war — evil Germany in-vading poor, brave, little Belgium. Noble Britain fighting to protect Belgium and fighting against the German barbari-ties of poisoned gas and zeppelins. If Goodwin was correct, there were no good guys and bad guys like in the W.S. Hart movies at the nickelodeon. Britain was just as much to blame for the war as Germany, and my father had died for nothing. It was all too confusing.

"I don't know," I said helplessly.

"Will," Goodwin went on quietly. "You're intelligent, that's not the problem. You've grown up within the system and no one has ever told you anything else. But try and step back and look at the war anew. If there is any truth to what I have been saying, then there are only two choices. Either you can support the war, and the system that makes it and all the misery it creates, or you can say that war is bad. If you say the latter, then your only choice is to try and change the system that created the war. That may not be easy and there may be a lot of pain involved, but what alternative is there?"

I couldn't answer that question. "It's so complicated."

"No," Goodwin said smiling, "it's not complicated at all. It's just that the ideas are new to you. All new ideas are frightening, especially if they are threatening, and social-ism, whether it is against the war or not, is threatening. It's all a question of power and who has it."

Goodwin paused, but I didn't have the strength to say anything, so he went on.

"The businessmen in England and Germany have the power. So they can control the war. But look at the situation in the mines here in Cumberland, it's just the same on a smaller scale.

"The coal company has power because it has a lot of money. If it gets in trouble, it can buy itself out of it. It has the power of life and death over its workers. The only way to change things is for the workers to get power from the company. The company doesn't want to give power to the workers, so the workers have to fight for it.

"One way to do that is by organizing into unions. A group of people are much stronger than a single person. If everyone in the mine refuses to work, then the company has to take notice. Unfortunately, the company can usually buy their way out of that problem. They can pay to bring in special police to break up union meetings, arrest union leaders, and force the workers' families out of the company houses. They can also bring in strikebreakers who are not part of the union and who will work to keep the mine going while the strike is on. There are not many workers who can stay on strike when they see that the mine is still working without them and their children are starving.

"The only way unions can be effective is if there is only one big union for everybody, whether they are coal miners, textile workers, or railroad workers. That way there won't be any strikebreakers and a strike can spread until it is too big for even the companies to buy their way out. Then there will be real change."

"Revolution," I said quietly.

"Yes," Goodwin added, "revolution. But what's revolution? It's just change. The invention of the steam engine was a revolution. It led to trains and cars and all kinds of factories, and it made Britain the most powerful country in the world. Now it has completely revolutionized the entire world, but few complained. Why? Because it was a revolution that benefited the people with the power. A worker's revolution is hated because it would benefit the people without power. It all comes back to power. Only the people with power can change things."

"The government has power," I said.

"Yes," Goodwin agreed, "but the government's power comes from the rich, so they will always support the bosses. Some people believe that is the way for workers to get power, by organizing and voting in a government of working men. I don't believe that."

"Why?" I asked, finding myself intrigued despite myself.

"Because it is too slow. The people with power will see it coming and do everything they can to stop it — even if it means a civil war. Whichever way you look at the problem, there will be violence. Power is never given up voluntarily. If I fight against the war and the people who make war, soldiers will die because of it. I know that and it is a horrible responsibility. But I also have a responsibility to the millions of men who will die if I do nothing and the system goes on producing wars for the benefit of the rich and powerful."

I was exhausted. Goodwin's ideas were new and difficult. They seemed to make sense when he was saying them, but I had to think about it. I was still angry.

"I'm tired," I said, pulling my steaming damp clothes around me and lying down.

"Good idea," Goodwin said, "we should probably try and get some rest. I'll build up the fire." He went into the trees to collect more wood.

The rain had stopped now and the occasional star was glittering through the tattered clouds above our heads. I could feel Morag looking at me. I felt horribly embarrassed at my outburst. Too embarrassed to try and talk to Morag about it, and she remained silent across the fire. I lay shivering on the damp ground in my wet clothes.

Goodwin returned with some wood which he dumped on the ground.

"This should keep us going for awhile," he said adding logs to the fire. I felt the increased heat warm the side of my body closest to the roaring blaze. I settled down and tried to get comfortable.

"Goodnight, Will Ryan." Goodwin's voice came from the other side of the flames.

"Goodnight," I murmured. Morag remained silent.

I didn't fall asleep for a long time. I thought over all that had happened in the last two days. I didn't understand most of it, but at least I hadn't had a lot of spare time to think about my loneliness. And another odd thing struck me. For all the things Goodwin said that I didn't understand or agree with, it reminded me very much of my father. He too had talked about the war forcing us all to make choices and take sides. His choice had been different from Goodwin's, but did that make it better?

Eventually, I dozed off as snippets of Morag and Goodwin's conversation drifted across the fire. I heard Morag's sister's name mentioned, but I was too tired to concentrate. The ground was uncomfortable, my ankle hurt, and Uncle Charles and Aunt Sophie would be worrying about me, but eventually I fell asleep.

All night I was plagued by dreams. My father was in many of them, but so was Goodwin. Sometimes I was in the trenches fighting; at others I was digging coal in the mine. In one, I was standing in an open, empty battlefield. To my left stood my father, beckoning me toward him. To my right stood Goodwin, asking me to come toward him. Straight in front stood Morag saying, "Go on. Don't be a coward. Make a choice." I awoke from that one in a sweat that had nothing to do with the heat from the fire. Goodwin and Morag were asleep. I stretched and went back to my disturbed dreams.

Monday, July 22, 1918

I awoke, stiff and sore, from my final patch of dream-filled sleep as the sun was just hauling itself above the distant peaks of the Coast Mountains. The sky was a fragile blue, and the few puffy, pink clouds bore no relation to their angry relatives that had made our lives such misery the night before. There was no sign of Morag, but Goodwin was sitting across the low fire.

"'Morning," he said cheerfully when he saw that I was awake.

"Good morning," I mumbled grudgingly. "Look, about last night. I . . ."

"Don't worry," he interrupted, "last night was then, this is now. How's your ankle?"

Sitting up, I experimentally moved my left foot. It was sore and I could see that the joint was swollen, but the pain was duller than last night.

"Not too bad," I replied.

"Good," he said, "I haven't got anything for breakfast and we should get you back to the boat and down the lake as soon as possible.

"I suppose even bosses worry about their families," he added with a mischievous look.

Morag appeared through the trees carrying some dead wood. She barely glanced at me. With the fire built up we warmed some of the aches out of our bones.

"Well," said Goodwin eventually, "I must be going. If I cannot pick up the supplies, I had better tell the others. I think we will lie low at Cougar Lake for a few days. We've got some supplies there. We'll try for a pickup next Saturday. And this time," Goodwin smiled at Morag, "I will check the post office first. Take care going back."

With that, Goodwin winked at us, turned, and disappeared into the woods. In silence, Morag and I rose and headed back down the slope. The going was slow and my ankle hurt with every step, but with care we made it to the lake shore in good shape. We took turns rowing over the calm water and were at the eagle tree by midmorning. The journey had been in a tense silence. Morag was obviously still angry, but I didn't want to leave it that way between us.

"Morag," I began tentatively, after she had stepped out of the boat, "I'm sorry about last night."

"Why?" she asked, dismissively. "It wasn't me you called a coward."

"Look, I've said I'm sorry. I was angry and confused. This is not easy for me, trying to settle into a new life here."

"A boss's life," she interrupted. "You can't understand the other point of view."

"That's not fair, I'm trying. I want to understand what's going on and make sense of it all. It wasn't my fault I wasn't born a coal miner's son. How would you like to lose your parents and be shunted half way around the world and dropped in a strange place where you don't know anyone?"

Morag didn't even reply. I watched in silence as she strode away into the trees. So much for all my dreams of an idyllic trip up the lake. I felt as though I had no control over my emotions. Whether I was happy or sad, angry or calm, depended on what Red Goodwin said or on Morag's mood. The former I could handle, at least Goodwin tried to explain his point of view; it was Morag's moods I found most difficult. They seemed irrational and, if I was honest with myself, I desperately wanted her to like me.

Despondently, I rowed back to the cabin.

Uncle Charles was at the mine, but Aunt Sophie was home. She had been worried, and fussed over me endlessly. My ankle was strapped up and I was fed hot soup and put into bed. That was where I spent the afternoon, sleeping, eating and feeling luxurious. By evening, my ankle was feeling much better, but I had a horrible cold. I was sitting up in bed with a towel over my head, sniffing a foul concoction of balsam and herbs that Aunt Sophie had prepared to clear my nose, when Uncle Charles returned.

"So you're safe," he said when he came in.

"Yes," I snuffled, "a bit sore, but all right."

My uncle nodded. "That was quite the storm. You were lucky you weren't caught out on the lake."

It was my turn to nod.

"I don't suppose you caught the giant trout?" he asked, sitting on the end of my bed and smiling.

"No," I admitted, "we didn't have much time to fish between Warren stopping us on the river and the storm."

Uncle Charles looked at me hard for the longest time. I was beginning to feel nervous when he went on. "So, Warren stopped you again. The man is a pest, but perhaps he's what we need to catch those deserters.

"How'd you sprain your ankle?" he asked, abruptly changing the subject.

"I was hurrying to get back to the boat before the storm arrived and I slipped."

"Close to the boat?" This was turning into an interrogation.

"Not too far up the river."

"Those sprains really hurt at first. I slipped once out in the bush surveying for the Number Four Mine. I've never known such pain. I couldn't put any weight on my leg at all."

My uncle paused reflectively. I relaxed as he rambled on

about his own accident. "I was only a couple of hundred yards from the road, but I doubt if I could have made it if one of the men hadn't been there to help me. Your sprain probably isn't that bad."

"No," I agreed, "and Morag helped . . ."

The look on Uncle Charles's face told me immediately that I'd made a serious mistake.

"Morag," he said thoughtfully. "That wouldn't be Morag McLean, by any chance would it?"

I nodded. What was the point in lying now? My uncle's face was deadly serious and I expected a violent blow-up, but when he spoke again it was in a terrifyingly calm voice.

"I wondered if it might be her when you talked about Warren stopping 'us' on the river." So mentioning Morag's name hadn't been my first mistake. "I'm frightfully disappointed in you, Will."

"But Uncle," I stuttered, hoping to make up some story to make things easier on myself.

But he would have none of it. "Silence! When I'm done you may correct me if I have made any serious errors of fact, but I doubt it will be necessary. You began by lying to me about going after some giant fish. I thought you looked frightened when I suggested coming with you. You had the trip already planned and knew I'd disapprove of your associating with that troublemaker McLean's daughter."

My silence was agreement.

"So, the only question now is how much you lied. Was it

lust alone that motivated you, or was there a darker purpose? If it was the former, why go to the trouble of going all the way down the lake? The woods are thick enough here for any disgusting activity to go unnoticed a few feet from the path."

My uncle paused thoughtfully. I could feel him looking at me, but I couldn't meet his eye.

"Where did Warren stop you on the lake yesterday when he stole your fish?"

"A bit down from the mouth of the river," I mumbled.

"And would that bit be about where the McLeans' cabin is?"

I said nothing.

"Everyone knows that the McLeans are supplying the deserters. So you warned them through the girl." Uncle Charles was speaking slowly now, forming his ideas as he spoke. It wasn't accurate, but I couldn't bring myself to deny it. It was close enough to the truth.

"I doubt if the cabin is the only place those men visit. If Warren was there, then a message would have to be left warning them to avoid it. That's why you gave me that cock-and-bull story about a giant fish and why you went up the lake with the McLean girl. Either you're very stupid and she is using you, or else you're deliberately helping those traitors. I can only hope it is the former, because I cannot imagine what your father would say if he were alive and knew that you were consciously helping men who were as responsible as the Germans for his death."

I shuddered at his words. They were unfair, but they hurt. I could feel tears forming. But my uncle wasn't finished yet.

"I take it from your silence that I am not too far from the truth. Well then, I will have to think what to do. You are a bit old for a beating, so I'll have to give your discipline some thought. Certainly it'll involve never going out again on that lake in my boat. Meanwhile, you lie there and think on your sins."

I did, for hours, as the twilight deepened to darkness and long after. I lay sweating, sneezing, coughing, and crying far into the night. I prayed that I was somewhere else, anywhere else. I cursed John Cabot for ever finding this country and I cursed my grandfather for sending me here. I wished all kinds of evils on Red Goodwin's head for making my life so complicated and for turning Morag against me. I blamed my father for dying and setting in train the events that led here, but most of all, I yearned to have him back. Eventually, I fell into a fevered sleep.

Tuesday/Wednesday,
July 23/24, 1918

—~w~—

The following two days are a blur in my memory. My cold became a fever and kept its grip on me as I lay, alternately sweating and shivering, drifting in and out of sleep. Aunt Sophie flitted worriedly about, ministering to me as best she could. I was forced to inhale foul-smelling concoctions and have all manner of pungent salves rubbed on my chest. Cold cloths were continually applied to my forehead to reduce my temperature, but little seemed to work.

I remember isolated images: the sound of my uncle noisily preparing to go to work, the hushed tones of my aunt talking with the doctor about influenza, and oddly the morning songs of the birds outside my window. But the patches of reality were swamped by my delirious dreams.

In my most vivid dream there is of a knock on the door. I don't think I said come in, but the door opened slowly to reveal my father in his officer's uniform.

"Dad! How did you get here? Aren't you dead?"

A slow smile crossed my father's face. It was exactly how he looked when we were playing games. An ache lay, like a huge knot in my stomach. I felt warm tears flowing down my cheeks.

"No," my father said, "I'm not dead. I was only wounded. The German miners dug me out of the tunnel, tended to my wounds and took me to a prison camp. I knew you would be worried, so I escaped. I was hidden by a Belgian family in Brussels until I could make it to Holland and sneak on a neutral ship for Britain. I arrived after you had been sent away and I followed you here."

"Why didn't you telegram that you were alive?"

"Because I wanted my arrival to be a surprise. It is, isn't it?"

"Yes," I said. "It's the most wonderful surprise in the world."

"As soon as you are better, we will go back to Britain. I am done with the war now and it will soon be over in any case. We will win, Germany will be taught a lesson, and you and I will play cricket in the back garden. Would you like that?"

"Yes!" I repeated. "Yes! Yes! Yes!"

My father stepped towards me. As he did so, he slowly faded and was replaced by Aunt Sophie. Reality reasserted itself.

"Shh," she said, "calm down and try to sleep."

"Father," I choked, overwhelmed by disappointment that it had only been a dream. I drifted off again.

In another dream I was tied to a medieval torture rack. Dan Warren was asking questions and turning the wheel if I refused to answer.

"Where is Red Goodwin hiding?"

"I don't know." Warren turned the wheel and pain shot through every joint in my body.

"When is he coming back down to collect supplies?"

"I don't know." More excruciating pain.

"It doesn't matter. I know where he is. I'll get him, dead or alive."

I struggle to get up. To escape and warn Ginger, but Warren vanished and the rack turned into a feather mattress, floating on the lake. As I revelled in the comfort, Morag mopped my brow.

"Morag," I sighed.

"Shh," she said. "It's all right now."

I was unutterably happy. But there was a worm of thought eating at the back of my mind. Something I had to do, or say.

"Morag!" I whispered breathlessly. "You must warn Ginger. Get a message to him at Cougar Lake. Tell him not to come down to the big rock on the Cruikshank on Saturday. It's too dangerous."

"I'll do that," Morag said. " Don't worry. I'm not angry any more."

There were a lot more dreams, the irrational attempts of my confused brain to make sense of all that was happening. But by Wednesday evening the dreams had faded, I was feeling much better. I was still incredibly weak, but my fever was down and I was hungry, always a good sign according to Aunt Sophie. She made me some chicken broth which I ate as I listened to the conversation coming from the adjoining room.

"I think he's come out of it," Aunt Sophie said.

"Yes," Uncle Charles agreed.

"I think he has suffered enough," my aunt went on.

"Perhaps." Uncle Charles didn't sound very convinced. "I suppose it is hard on the boy. I meant what I said about the boat, and we'll have to keep a very close rein on him. He mustn't start hanging around with that McLean girl and the wrong sort of people. We have a responsibility after all. But I won't give him any more of a discipline." There was silence for a moment, then Uncle Charles went on.

"There was an accident today," he said, "down in Number Four deep level." I was immediately alert.

"Oh dear," Aunt Sophie said, "was anyone hurt?"

"Yes," my uncle replied, "a Chinaman was injured. There was movement along one of the fractures and a piece of the roof came down — crushed the man's legs. Only took a few hours to clear the rubble and shore up the roof, but it's still time lost and any reduction in output is serious when the pressure's on to increase our shipments. Damned bad luck. These things always seem to happen at the worst possible time."

I lay horrified at my uncle's callousness. He seemed to care only about mine production not that a man had been crushed. I couldn't help comparing his attitude to Goodwin's when he talked about soldiers or miners being killed.

I lay awake thinking, but when I did fall into a dream-free sleep, it was the best night's rest I'd had for days.

Thursday, July 25, 1918

—⁓—

I awoke feeling almost human. I had a deep, chesty cough, and my body felt as if it had been severely beaten, but my ankle had benefited from the enforced rest and was much better. My mood, however, was still black. I felt strangely detached from the events of the past few days. Even what I knew to be reality, like the night on the ridge in the storm, seemed more like a dream. On the other hand, the delirious hallucinations of my dead father's visit and my torture seemed like reality. At least now my head was clear.

I stayed in bed until I heard Uncle Charles leave for work. I had no wish to talk to him just yet. I dressed and limped through to the kitchen where Aunt Sophie was working at the sink.

"Good morning," she said as I entered. "How are you feeling?"

"Not too bad," I said truthfully. "A bit weak and hungry."

"Good," she said, bustling over to the pantry, "a good breakfast will set you up. Bacon, eggs and sourdough bread all right?"

"Lovely," I said sitting myself at the rough table. "What day is it?"

"Thursday," my aunt replied as she put the fry pan on the large wood stove and loaded it with thick rashers of bacon. "You've been delirious for two whole days. We were very worried. You had a terrible fever and you were thrashing around and talking to yourself. We thought it was that Spanish Influenza that is so bad over in Europe at the moment, but the doctor said that it was just a fever from sleeping out in the storm." The bacon began to sizzle and the smell made my mouth water.

"Is Uncle Charles very angry?" I asked.

"Well," said Aunt Sophie thoughtfully, "he is not happy, that's for sure, but he'll get over it. He was just as worried about your sickness as me. Why, he spent the longest time sitting by your bed when you were ranting on so. I think you may have a lecture coming, and it will be a long time before you can go out in the boat, but that'll be all. Just be sure you don't go associating with any of those union troublemakers."

I nodded and began to tackle the mound of bacon, eggs

and bread that was placed before me. I was amazed at my appetite. I finished everything and then managed seconds. By the end, my trousers were uncomfortably tight, but I felt I could face the world once more.

"Thanks," I said, wiping my mouth. "I feel much better."

"Good," my aunt said happily. "Now, I am going to launder your bedding and air your room. Why don't you take a short stroll if you feel up to it? Some fresh air will do you good."

"Good idea," I said, standing and heading for the door.

"Don't go far," Aunt Sophie called after me, "I don't want to have to come looking for you and I am too old to carry you home."

"All right," I called back.

Walking slowly, and favouring my sore ankle, I made my way through the trees to the log where I had talked to Morag five days ago. It was going to be a hot day, but it hadn't warmed up yet and the air was fresh and cool. I took deep breaths and felt glad to be out of bed.

I sat down to rest on the log — and think. So much had happened in the past few days. Until that week, things hadn't been too bad. I had been unsettled and upset at finding myself in this strange world, but I had managed to put some distance between it and me. I had been an observer, watching and learning about the landscape and the people, but I hadn't been involved. The problems of the miners and the bosses, the "war" as Goodwin called it, hadn't affected me directly and I had assumed that they never would. I would live my life here as long as I had to, and as soon as possible I would return and make my life in Britain.

Now, all that had changed. I had been drawn in, mostly against my will, to become involved in circumstances I barely understood. I wasn't a revolutionary or a policeman, but both were rapidly becoming important in my life. I had to live with Uncle Charles and I wanted friendships with Morag and Jimmy Wong, but that didn't seem to be possible. Friendship required involvement in the complexities of people's lives. The horrible thing was that all three of the people who were important in my life at that moment, wanted different things from me, and I couldn't satisfy them all. I would have to make a choice.

I was wondering about this when I heard a noise on the trail. Looking up, I saw Jimmy Wong standing before me, frowning.

"Hello Jimmy," I said.

"Have you talked to your uncle about the gas?" he asked without preamble.

"A bit," I stuttered, guilt at not being more forceful with Uncle Charles sweeping over me.

"A bit?" Jimmy's voice was heavy with irony. "What do you mean by that?"

"He brought the subject up," I explained weakly.

"Oh, well that's all right then. And what did he say when he brought the subject up?"

"He said it was probably nothing."

"Probably nothing," Jimmy repeated sarcastically. "Well that's a relief then. Probably just some damned, lazy China-man wanting a holiday. Good that you had a pleasant chat about it. I don't know why I expected anything else."

I cringed at the harshness of his words, shocked that someone I regarded as a friend could be so cruel. Obviously the "war" in Cumberland cut across the bonds of friendship.

"Do you know there was an accident yesterday?" Jimmy went on.

"Yes. A piece of roof came down, didn't it."

"It did, but it's not serious. It was cleared away in a few hours. It didn't delay production by much."

"But someone was injured."

"Only a Chink. He was number 372. He was taking lunches down to the face. The rock landed on his legs, crushing them from the thighs down."

The anger in Jimmy's words hit me like physical blows.

"Will they have to amputate?" I asked.

"No."

"No? But you said . . ."

"They won't have to do anything. Chinaman number 372 died at five this morning."

I saw tears pooling in Jimmy's eyes. Abruptly, he spun around and began walking back down the trail.

"Wait," I shouted, standing up and limping after him. "What was his name?"

Jimmy stopped and turned. His head tilted to one side and he looked hard at me. Tears ran down his cheeks. "Sam. His name was Sam Guen. He liked to play football. He was seventeen. He was my friend."

"I'm sorry," I said, but it sounded terribly inadequate.

"So am I, but Sam's death is minor."

"What do you mean?"

"The piece of rock fell because the pressure is building up in the deep shaft. It's the same pressure that is pushing the gas out into the tunnels. When the gas explodes, and it will sooner or later, the explosion could trigger a major cave-in. Hundreds of miners might be killed. And what's being done? Nothing." The anger was rising in Jimmy's voice again.

"I'll talk to uncle Charles again," I offered.

"No. That won't do any good. If anything is going to be done, we will have to do it. Father has a plan. You stay here, safe and comfortable."

I didn't have a chance to protest or ask what he meant, before Jimmy's face softened. "I'm sorry. That was unfair. This is not your struggle. It's not your fault your uncle won't do anything."

Jimmy walked away, but after three steps he stopped and turned back. "Sam's funeral is tomorrow afternoon," he said, then he was gone down the trail.

I went back to my log and sat down. I was exhausted, from the illness and from the emotional turmoil created by talking to Jimmy. I felt so helpless. Jimmy was right, talking to Uncle Charles would do no good. There was nothing I could do.

Or was there? Had Jimmy offered me a chance to do something? Was he testing me? Did he want me to go to the funeral tomorrow to prove there was at least one white person who saw Sam Guen as more than a number? I didn't know, but I determined then to go to the funeral.

For the remainder of Thursday I rested and Aunt Sophie fussed. When Uncle Charles came back that evening, I got the promised lecture, which I received in silence. As soon as possible, I excused myself and went to bed where I lay thinking about the strange turns my already confused life had taken in the past few days. Then I fell asleep.

Friday, July 26, 1918

AFTERNOON

———~~~———

I slept late and awoke feeling almost completely better. My ankle still ached a bit but, apart from a slight limp, I could get about as well as ever. After a good-sized combination breakfast and lunch, I excused myself by telling Aunt Sophie that I was going for a walk to get some fresh air and exercise. Then I headed into town. The most direct route cut inland from the lake, along the ridge behind Number Four Mine. I had just passed the mine when a small Chinese man, hunched over and obviously in a hurry, passed. I recognized Jimmy's father and said hello, but Mr. Wong was either too deep in thought or in too much of a hurry to reply.

As I neared Cumberland, I began to wonder how I would find the funeral in the warren of streets in Chinatown. I needn't have worried. To reach the Chinese cemetery, the funeral had to pass through Cumberland, and the cacophony of bells, cymbals and a brass band announced what was going on long before I reached Dunsmuir Avenue.

The procession was heading east, down the hill, and at first I didn't realize that it was a funeral. I thought there must be a parade going on at the same time. It seemed much too noisy, colourful and cheerful. Knots of people lined both sides of the street and I was relieved to see several curious white faces. On the one hand, I had wanted to be the only white person there, to show Jimmy that I was different from all the rest. On the other hand, I was scared of standing out and attracting too much attention. I moved between the people until I got a good view.

I had been too young to remember my mother's funeral, but I was certain it had been nothing like this. I had expected muted colours, bowed heads and quiet sadness. But it was colourful lanterns, banners and umbrellas floating above the procession. Several of the mourners were dressed in white or wore white headbands. The brass band was making the most noise, but many people were clashing small cymbals or ringing hand bells. I had no idea what was happening; the whole spectacle seemed garish and strange. A riderless white horse was being led past when I heard a familiar voice over my shoulder.

"Come to gawk at the Chinks?" Even when it was insulting me, Morag's voice sent a shiver down my spine.

"No," I said, turning to face her, "I've come to pay my respects to Sam Guen."

Morag looked confused. "How do you know his name?"

"Jimmy told me. He doesn't always assume the worst about people."

Morag stared hard at me for a long moment. Then her face softened. "Do you know what's going on?" she asked.

"I have no idea," I replied. "It's not like any funeral I have ever seen. It seems too . . . cheerful."

The faintest of smiles flitted across Morag's lips. "It is not cheerful. The people are in deep mourning."

"But the bright colours and the music and bells?"

"Sam's family is Buddhist. White is the colour of mourning for them. The other colours all mean something too. I don't know them all, but if Sam had had children they would wear black, grandchildren blue and so on. Colour is very important. For example, the body must never be dressed in red or else it will return as a ghost."

"What about the horse?"

"That carries Sam's spirit so he doesn't have to walk. And do you see those men in tall hats? They are to ward off evil spirits."

The men in hats were followed by several more carrying banners with Chinese characters on them. "What do those say?" I asked.

"I can't read Chinese," Morag answered, "but they probably say something about Sam's life. You see the banners have the eight auspicious signs marked on them."

I peered, and sure enough there were pictures painted on the banners, I recognized a fish, an umbrella, a jar of some kind and a shell. The others just confused me. The hearse was now going past with the coffin on the back. It was followed by people I assumed were Sam's family, each wearing a white headband. Many of them carried ordinary household objects.

"Why are they carrying those things?"

"Those are things that were important to Sam. They will be burned after the funeral as will all of Sam's clothes and those the mourners are wearing."

Behind the family, the procession was completed by a small group of young people. I recognized Jimmy amongst them. He was wearing a white headband and carrying a football. As he passed, he looked up and nodded slightly at us. Then the procession was gone and the crowd dispersed.

"Should we go up to the cemetery?" I asked.

"No, that is just for family. Not even Jimmy's going to that ceremony.

"Look, Will, I'm sorry I got so mad at you up the lake the other day. Things seem to be spinning out of control all of a sudden. It used to be a game, but now, with Warren and the others here, it has become much more complicated and serious. I'm scared about what is going to happen."

"It's okay," I said with a smile, "I know how you feel. I've been feeling much the same ever since I arrived here." I was rewarded with a smile. Encouraged, I continued. "Are you going up the lake tonight?"

"Shh!" Morag glanced around quickly. She looked worried even though there was no one close to us. "Be careful what you say."

I thought Morag was worrying unnecessarily, but I decided not to say anything more. The silence lengthened as I searched for something else to say that would keep the conversation going. Morag kept glancing around. Eventually, she pointed along the street. "Here he comes," she said.

I followed her arm and saw Jimmy threading his way through the people on the boardwalk. He no longer carried the football and he had removed the white bandanna from his head. Obviously, Morag and Jimmy's meeting was pre-arranged. I wondered if my presence had been planned too, but then Jimmy was beside us. He nodded to Morag and then looked at me. "Thanks for coming," he said. "Now, let's go."

"Where?" I asked as the pair set off.

"Didn't you tell him?" Jimmy asked Morag.

"No. I thought you had."

"We're going to the mine," Jimmy said to me. "Father has something planned to make the deep shaft safe."

"I saw him heading to the mine on my way here. He was in a hurry."

Jimmy nodded acknowledgment and set off with Morag close behind. I had a lot of unanswered questions, but if I wanted answers I had no choice but to follow.

I had to hurry to keep up along the rough track to the mine. My ankle held up well, although I had to concentrate not to turn it in one of the deep cart ruts. The last thing I wanted to do was twist it again. As we strode along, I wondered at the strange turn of events. I didn't understand what was happening, but I was pleased to be included.

Friday, July 26, 1918

EVENING

—✳—

By the time we reached the pithead it was late afternoon. A crowd was gathered and something unusual was obviously going on. About a hundred Chinese men stood in a confused knot in front of the wooden trestle that carried the coal from the head frame at the top of the deep shaft to the tipple where it was sorted. They were huddled in a tight group, like a school of fish that sticks together for mutual protection. What they needed protection from was a smaller group of about thirty white miners who were standing to one side angrily shaking their fists and shouting insults at the Chinese men.

"What's happening?" I asked as we stopped at the edge of the clearing.

"They've stopped work," Jimmy said, obvious pride in his voice. "My father has persuaded them to down picks and leave the coal face."

"Because of the gas," Morag added, although I had already worked that part out.

"What will happen now?"

"I don't know," Jimmy said, a puzzled note entering his voice. "I can't see father anywhere. He told me he was going to get them out and then bargain for a gas test."

Jimmy edged towards the cluster of men, and Morag and I were pulled along behind him. I was suddenly overcome by the sense that we were entering a different world. It wasn't just the angry shouts of the men in front of us; the entire landscape had an unreal quality to it. The backdrop to the scene was a dark mass of tree-covered hills, which extended almost down to the trestle. The trestle itself, made from an assortment of logs many of which were only partly stripped of bark, looked as if it had been thrown together by an insane giant. Irregular wooden buildings framed the clearing on either side, some windowless, others with glassless holes. Many had crude, blackened chimneys out of which belched grey smoke.

The clearing itself looked devastated. Huge charred stumps, some taller than me, were scattered about. Equipment, apparently discarded, lay everywhere — a wagon wheel against a stump, the axle from a coal car, a holed steam boiler and stacked logs. The only regularity in the view was the railroad track running diagonally across the scene.

As we picked our way closer, I began to hear what was being shouted. It was not pleasant.

"Get back to work."

"Damned lazy Chinks."

"Why don't you go home if you're too chicken to go underground?"

Some of the white miners carried clubs or held rocks in their hands. I felt the tension. It was only inches away from bursting into violence. Nervously, I fell back as Jimmy approached the Chinese group. He spoke to one of the men who handed him a sheet of paper. Jimmy turned to us with a confused look on his face.

"He says that my father went back into the mine. Why would he do that?"

Morag and I shrugged as Jimmy rejoined us. "He needs to be here to speak for the men. They won't stay out without someone to lead them. He left this letter for me." Jimmy looked down at the folded paper in his hand.

"What the bloody hell is going on here?" I swung around to see Uncle Charles and two other men stride around the side of the trestle. All three were wearing suits and bowler hats and looked oddly out of place amongst the men in working clothes and against the devastated landscape. "What is this shift doing on the surface when there is coal to be dug?"

One of the white miners stepped forward. He was dressed in a coarse jacket and pants. The pants were tied at the ankles and waist with string, and everything, including his shirt and face, were black with coal dust. Only his eyes looked white. Like the others, he carried a large, round lunch pail and wore a flat cap with a stiff brim to which a small lantern was fastened. As he stepped forward, he removed his cap with his free hand.

"It wass thae Chinese," he said in a strong Scottish Highland accent. "All of a sudden, they up and refuses to work, chust like that. It wass yon Wong who stirred them all up. We could dae nothin' but follow them oot. Mind, there iss gass in the deep shaft for shure."

"Where's Wong?" my uncle demanded, looking around and ignoring the miner's final comment. He noticed us for the first time. I cringed under his angry gaze. "What the devil are you doing here? Don't I have enough trouble without children sticking their noses in where they are not wanted?

"You," he said, pointing at Jimmy, "Where's your father?"

"I don't know," Jimmy replied. His voice was firm but quiet. "The men say he went back into the mine."

"What the hell for?"

Jimmy shrugged.

"Well, it doesn't matter," Uncle Charles continued, turning to the group of miners, "what matters is getting you lot back to work. Now, if you want to see another pay cheque, you'll get back underground and finish your shift."

The Chinese men stirred uneasily. A few of them began to drift toward the shaft entrance. Without a leader, they were helpless.

I don't know why I suddenly remembered something

Jimmy had told me by the lake the day before. He had said that his father had a plan. He had repeated it in town on the way here. Why I should have connected that to the letter Jimmy had been given, I have no idea, but all of a sudden a chill ran down my spine. I had a horrible premonition. Instinctively, I stepped forward. "No!" I shouted. Morag and Jimmy, Uncle Charles and the shuffling miners all stopped and looked at me. I had their attention, but what was I going to say?

"It's dangerous. There's gas."

"Not this nonsense again," Uncle Charles said. "I'll talk to you later, young man, now the rest of you get back to work."

"You mustn't," I jumped onto a nearby stump. It was vital that I stop the men going back into the mine, but I couldn't explain it to them. What could I say? In a flash, I remembered Ginger Goodwin standing on a stump in the wilderness. "There's a war going on," I shouted, waving my arms. I had their attention now. I didn't know where I was going, but it didn't matter, I had to keep talking. As long as they stayed and listened to me they were safe. I used Goodwin's words. "You are being fooled by the company. Long hours and unsafe practices are killing miners as surely as German bombs and bullets are killing soldiers in Flanders."

I was aware of Jimmy and Morag standing beside me open-mouthed. I was acting to impress Morag as much as the miners. I made a sweeping gesture, but was careful not to step too close to the edge of the stump. "There is gas down there and it will explode. Men will be killed unless testing is done. Mister Wong knows that."

That was when Jimmy realized what his father was doing. With an incoherent shout, he raced forward towards the open mine shaft.

"Now look," my uncle yelled. "What the . . ."

He was interrupted by a deep thump from beneath our feet. It wasn't loud and was felt as much as heard, but the miners knew what it meant. As one man, they turned to look at the dark shaft entrance. Jimmy stopped about fifteen feet from the black hole. For an age nothing happened, then a cloud of dirty grey smoke billowed out of the shaft. It swirled around Jimmy and dispersed into the air.

"Oh my God!" Uncle Charles exclaimed.

"Father!" Jimmy shouted and leapt forward. I think he would have rushed headlong into the mine but the white miner who had spoken to Uncle Charles grabbed him.

"Dinnae be a bloody fool," he said. Then over his shoulder, "Jack, go for the Draegermen, ass fast ass you can."

The next few hours, until they brought Jimmy's father's body out, were a chaos of quiet emotion. The miners milled about, talking in subdued tones and glancing uneasily at the shaft entrance where five men dressed in cumbersome breathing apparatus had disappeared.

The "bump," as an underground explosion is called, had been felt in town and soon drew worried family members to the mine. Scenes of tearful relief were played out in the clearing all afternoon.

In all the confusion, the three of us were ignored. Jimmy

had been brought over to us by the miner who had stopped him running into the mine.

"Lass, you see ass how he'll no dae onythin' daft," he had said to Morag. Then he turned to me. "That wass a fine way to mak' a speech."

Jimmy sat hunched over, his head in his hands, shoulders convulsed by sobs. Morag and I tried our best to console him. At length he raised his head and looked at us in red-eyed misery. "He had it all planned," he said disconsolately. "But he didn't have to die. He had got the men out of the mine. Why did he go back in?"

I thought I knew the answer, but while I was thinking what to say, Jimmy seemed to notice the letter from his father still clutched in his hand. Morag and I watched in silence as he unfolded it and read. Then he passed it over to us.

Jimmy.

By the time you read this, I will be dead. It is my hope that no one else will.

I am afraid I have had to lie to you. You know of my plan to get the men out of the mine, but that alone will not be enough. We are not organized or determined enough. We need a strong leader and I am not that man. I do not have the oratory to make men do my wishes. Therefore, getting the men out is not enough. Mister Ryan and the white miners will put pressure on them and they will return, despite anything I can do. The only way is to show them.

The gas is getting much worse and I think it is not far from an explosion. My plan is to clear the mine of the afternoon shift. I will then return underground and set off the explosion myself. That way there will be no disaster and Mister Ryan will have to believe what I said. I hope I am brave enough to carry this through.

I have left a letter for Mother with my papers in the tin box at the house. Please make sure she gets it. You have both made my life very happy. I could not have asked for a better family.

I have tried to do my best for you and to give you skills that will make your life better than mine. I know it will be difficult for you, stuck between two cultures as you are, but I hope you will not give up. If we are to live and prosper in this country, we must become like the people here. In time they will accept us, perhaps even within your lifetime.

I will leave this with the shift foreman. I wish it could be longer.

Look after your mother and make something of your life. Please try to forgive me for leaving you both.

Father

"Five hundred and thirty-two."

Morag and I looked at Jimmy.

"That was my father's number. He pulled himself up from being a coal face worker to be a representative for hundreds of men. He gave up the old ways, dressed and talked like a European, married a European wife and brought up a European son, but for all that, the mine records will still show that today Chinaman number 532 was killed in an accident underground."

There was nothing either Morag or I could think of saying to assuage Jimmy's bitterness.

"Nothing will change," Jimmy said quietly. "I might as well go down the mine."

"You can't!" I exclaimed. "What about school?"

"School," Jimmy scoffed dismissively. "What's the point of school? I'll end up a smart Chink, but I'll still be just a Chink, fit only to be given a number and to shovel coal. I don't need to read Shakespeare to do that. My father was a fool to think we can better ourselves."

"Don't ever say that," I said, "I never knew your father. I only ever saw him at a distance, but I know he was not a fool. He was a brave man who struggled for what he believed in. Like my father. Like Ginger Goodwin. They should be admired." I sensed Morag looking hard at me, but I kept my gaze on Jimmy. "The world is bigger than Robert Dunsmuir's little coal mining empire and not everyone is like my uncle. Don't throw everything you have away. I'm leaving this place as soon as I can. You should too."

"But you're white."

"Yes, I am white, but that's no guarantee of an easy life. If it were, I wouldn't be here and Ginger Goodwin wouldn't be hiding out in the hills."

"Perhaps," Jimmy said.

We sat in silence for a long while after that, each deep in his own thoughts. For myself, I thought of two things that I had only just come to realize.

The first was that I wasn't going to stay here. I had been sent because my grandfather had assumed that I needed an adult to look after me. I had gone along with it because it simply never occurred to me to think otherwise. Now I had seen boys my age who worked a ten-hour day at a coal face deep below the earth, and I knew that there were soldiers as young as me dying in France. I didn't need Uncle Charles and Aunt Sophie to look after me. I had grown up a lot in the past weeks and I could look after myself. I wasn't going to go down the mines or join the army, but there was a lot I could do if I had the courage to try it. Canada was a big place.

The second was that I didn't hate Ginger Goodwin — I admired him. On the stump, I had instinctively quoted him and I had given him as an example of bravery in the same breath as my father.

I looked over at Morag. Her face was in profile to me and she was deep in thought. She was so beautiful. An insane idea swept through my mind: Morag and I could run away together. At that moment, Morag looked around and smiled at me. All my doubts and confusion vanished. I smiled back and opened my mouth. Before I could say anything, we were distracted by a movement of the groups of men towards the mine shaft.

"They've found him," Jimmy said.

Feeling guilty that I had so easily forgotten Jimmy's pain, I followed the other two over towards the cluster of men.

The Draegermen stood in a tight knot just outside the shaft entrance. Their breathing apparatus hung over their shoulders and their faces bore expressions of tired resignation. Four of them carried a stretcher on which lay a blanket-draped body. Jimmy stepped forward and reached for the corner of the blanket. A Draegermen reached over and held his wrist.

"I wouldn't," he said. "He was right at the flash point of the explosion. He couldn't have felt anything, but the heat . . . His face . . ."

The man's voice trailed off and Jimmy dropped his arm.

A sudden scream tore our attention away from the scene around the stretcher. A small woman forced herself forward. She wore a cotton print dress, the colourful flowers on the dress looking oddly out of place amidst the drab surroundings. Around her waist was an apron still with flour stains on it. Her face was contorted into ugliness by her grief. It was the first time I had seen Jimmy's mother.

The crowd parted to let her through. Jimmy grabbed her before she could hurl herself at the stretcher.

"No, Mom," he said gently. "There's nothing we can do."

The woman collapsed sobbing into Jimmy's arms. Everyone suddenly seemed embarrassed by the outpouring of emotion from this small woman that I had heard many of them call a whore for marrying a Chinaman. Eventually, the leader of the white miners stepped forward.

"Come on, lass," he said. "The missus and the ither women iss over at the shack wi' a grand pot o' tea." He took Jimmy's arm and led the pair away from the shaft. A collective sigh went around the gathered men, and many began talking in hushed tones. The Draegermen and their burden headed towards a hut with a large red cross crudely painted on one wall. The miners began to disperse. I looked around, but could see no sign of my uncle. Shouldn't he be here at a time like this? I felt a soft touch on my arm.

"Let's go," Morag said. "There's no point in staying here."

We walked back across the clearing.

"Did you really mean that?" Morag asked.

"Mean what?"

"What you said about admiring Ginger."

"Yes, I did," I replied. "I may not agree with all his ideas, but I admire him for standing up for what he believes in. One thing I have learned here is that life is not all black and white. Perhaps the pacifists are right and all we can do is decide not to fight for anything at all.

"And there's something else."

Morag stopped walking over the rutted ground and looked at me. We had reached one of the rough shacks on the edge of the mine clearing. My mind was a swirl of emotion. Morag was standing very close to me. The dryness in my throat made it difficult to speak.

"I'm not going to stay here. In three weeks time I'll be seventeen, old enough to look after myself. I have nothing in common with Uncle Charles and, in any case, he just sees me as a burden. I don't want to work in the mines, either as a miner or a boss. There is nothing for me here."

"Nothing?" Morag stepped even closer. I could feel her breath on my cheek.

"I mean . . . Well . . ." I stammered. Then she kissed me, full on the lips. All my plans melted. In that moment I would have agreed to stay and dig coal, or go to war, or climb Mount Everest — whatever she asked me. Suddenly, Cumberland with its filthy, ravaged landscape, was the best place on earth.

Morag drew back. I grinned like an idiot. She smiled.

"Morag I . . ." I was going to ask her to run away with me, but I never got the chance. The door on the far side of the hut we were beside slammed. We both jumped. I recognized my uncle's voice. "About bloody time, Warren."

Morag and I froze, our smiles replaced by frowns. Slowly we leaned towards the wall of the hut, as much to hide as to better hear what was being said inside.

"Yeah, well it's a busy life being a cop. I'm leading a posse up the lake tomorrow to finish this thing. Some of the boys found a cache this morning, some clothes, an old pair of boots and a rifle. We're close to catching these fellows. Now, what is it you want to tell me?"

"Look, Warren, I don't like you, but I realize you have a

job to do and that it must be done. I have some information that you'll find useful but I want you to know that I'm only giving it to you so that you can do your work and then get out of our town as quickly as possible."

"Okay, so I won't hold my breath waiting for the invite round for drinks and dinner. What information do you have?"

There was a long pause inside as if my uncle was wrestling with whether to speak or not. When he did, his words sent a chill down my spine.

"Goodwin and the others aren't camped up the Cruikshank; they're over by Cougar Lake." Morag tensed beside me.

"That's rough country back in there," Warren said.

"Yes," my uncle agreed, "but they have to come over to the Cruikshank to fish and collect supplies. There's a drop-off point at the big rock about two miles up the river. My guess is that is where the supplies are left, too. Some are going up tomorrow."

"How do you know all this?"

There was another long pause. "My nephew told me."

I gasped in horror. Morag stepped back, a puzzled look on her face.

"I didn't . . . I don't know . . ." I began in an urgent whisper, but where could I go after that? I was as confused as she was.

Morag shook her head questioningly. "Will? Did you?"

Suddenly it all came clear. That was why Uncle Charles had been so attentive when I was sick. I had been talking out loud in my wild dreams. I had betrayed Ginger, even if I hadn't known I was doing it.

"I was delirious. I didn't know what I was saying."

Morag looked unutterably sad. I wanted to comfort her. I reached forward. Familiar anger flashed in her eyes. "I trusted you," she hissed. Then, turning on her heel, she strode off towards the trees.

I should have run after her, or shouted her name, but I didn't. I just slumped down miserably against the hut wall and wept.

I sat there in my anguish for a long time. I was vaguely aware of figures passing by, but no one paid me much attention. Eventually, a long shadow stopped by me and I heard a familiar voice.

"Haff you no' got a home tae go to, lad?"

I looked up to see the Scottish miner who had spoken up earlier. I shrugged disconsolately.

"Weel, I want to chust thank you fer yon speech. It might hae saved a life or twa. An' it wass a brave thing to dae wi' your uncle there. My daughter says that you twa dinna get on tae weel."

"Your daughter?"

"Aye. Morag. Did you no' ken? She's a fine lass, but auffy hot-heeded. She's aye frightenin' the wife wi' her antics. Fer example, she wauld think nothin' o' traipsin' up yon lake wi' a pack fu' o' supplies fer yon Goodwin fella. Mind, there's nothin' wrong wi' that, her heid's screwed on right enough, yon Goodwin's done a lot fer the miners hereabouts, but he hass nae sense o' caution. Wi' men like Warren aroon' it's tae dangerous fer a lass tae carry on like she's been daen'. It's bad enough wi' Goodwin showin' up at a' 'oors o' the night to pay court to Morag's sister, wi'oot her bein' caught wi' a pack fu' o' groceries. I'm thinkin' I'll be lockin' the doors and keepin' a close eye on thae twa girls the night. They'll no' be wanderin' aroon the woods fer the next few days.

"Anyhoo, I must be off, mysel'. Thank you, and keep your heid doon."

As I watched him pick his way into the distance, I tried to reconcile the soft-spoken man I had just met with the strike leader I knew Morag's father to be. His quiet way must hide a strong resolve. Perhaps that explained why he had not suffered more for his role in the big strike.

Nothing was simple in this place. Disconsolately, I headed back to the cabin. For the moment, I had nowhere else to go.

Friday, July 26/Saturday July 27, 1918

NIGHT

On the walk back, I toyed with the idea of running away — of stealing the boat and joining the deserters at the head of the lake, or of going even farther, jumping a ship and losing myself in the vastness of Canada or going down to San Francisco. Apart from being hungry, thirsty and tired, and having a dull pain in my ankle throb constantly and sap my strength, I knew I didn't fit in with Goodwin and the others. It would be embarrassing for both of us to have me suddenly show up and announce that I was going to live in the wilderness with them. As for running away to seek my fortune elsewhere, I was hardly prepared, and Friday evening was probably not the best time to start. In any case, I had to go back to tell Aunt Sophie that I was all right. She had been kind to me and I didn't want her worrying. Facing Uncle Charles was a less attractive prospect.

Aunt Sophie was pleased to see me and happily ladled out a generous helping of stew from the pot on the stove. She had heard something of events at the mine, but didn't know any details, and I was not about to fill her in. It never ceased to amaze me how Aunt Sophie managed to live in the middle of all that was going on in Cumberland and not seem to understand. She was generous, kind and would help anyone, miner, boss or Chinese labourer, who needed it, yet she never questioned the circumstances that produced the need.

"Terrible thing, that accident at the mine," she said as I tucked into my second plate of stew. "Those poor men working in those dreadful conditions. I don't know how they do it."

"I don't think they have much choice."

"Nonsense. Everyone has a choice. It's the children I feel sorry for. What kind of life do they have?"

"But what choice does a miner have? His house belongs to the mine, he is probably in debt at the company store, and he has to keep earning money just to keep food on the table for his children."

"Well, he shouldn't go on strike then for a start," Aunt Sophie went on. "What good does that do his children?"

"It can do some, if it gets him safer working conditions, shorter hours or a few pennies more a week."

"Piffle. What good did the Big Strike do? None. You weren't here, but I saw the women and children sitting begging by the road with no home but a canvas awning over their heads. Almost two years that went on and what did they get for all that suffering and anger? Nothing. If this is all the miners want, I don't know why they ever left Wales or Scotland or China or wherever they all come from."

I obviously wouldn't make a very good political leader. I couldn't even convince my aunt of something. On the other hand, she was a difficult person to argue with. She might not think very hard about the underlying causes of what she saw around her, but that didn't prevent her holding strong opinions. She also had the disconcerting habit of changing the topic. I would think I was talking about one thing and suddenly I would find that I was talking about something entirely different. It was a bit like trying to walk on quicksand, the ground kept moving beneath your feet. She went off on a tangent now.

"I loved the little house we had in Yorkshire before we came out here. It was so pretty, with roses all around the door and a beautiful view over the Dales. Of course, it was not anything as grand as your grandfather's place, but I loved it."

"Why did you and Uncle Charles come to Canada?" I asked, happy enough that the conversation had moved away from the mine.

"Oh, it was your Uncle Charles' idea. He never really got on with his father, your grandfather. Charles was too independent. He was always in favour of the new ideas and machinery — said it would change our world. Your grandfather would have none of that. He wanted things to go on forever just as they had under old Queen Victoria. On top of that, I don't think Charles' family quite approved of his marrying me. My family were grocers, you see. Successful, but not quite upper class enough for Charles' family.

"When Charles was courting me," Aunt Sophie went on wistfully, "he had all these wonderful ideas for a new life. At that time it was India. We would go out there and he would make a fortune in some business or other. Then it was New Zealand and sheep farming. Nothing came of his ideas, until we came here.

"Well, not here exactly. We went to the Northwest Territories first — what is Saskatchewan now. That would have been in 1904. This man, Reverend Barr, was offering farms for anyone who wanted them. Charles jumped at the chance, even though he had never farmed a day in his life. It wasn't what we expected, or what Barr promised for that matter, but there was nothing we could do. There we were, winter coming on and only a crude hut made out of sod bricks.

"That winter was hard. I never even guessed it could be so cold. When spring finally came, the man on the section next to ours offered to buy us out. He could see we would never make a go of it. So we took the little money he offered and came out here. At least the winters weren't so harsh. Charles got in with some people who knew his father from home and they helped him get experience and, eventually, this job."

"It's not much like farming."

"No, it's not," Aunt Sophie said with a sad smile, "and your uncle knows that. It's been hard on him, coming down from all his dreams. At least he has a good job here. I don't think I could stand the worry if he had to go underground. Perhaps one day we will have put enough by to move away to Victoria, or even out east to Toronto."

"Couldn't you go back to Britain?"

"No. Not with the war and all."

"But the war won't last forever."

"Sometimes I wonder," Aunt Sophie gazed out the window. "I think it might go on until all the young men are killed. Maybe those boys hiding up in the hills are right. At least they are alive.

"Anyway, Charles can't go home. What would he do? He has a position here. People look up to him. He wouldn't have that back home. He won't go home and admit that he failed in his dreams. Much better to stay here and write cheerful letters about how well we are doing." I saw a tear glisten on Aunt Sophie's cheek before she abruptly wiped her eyes on her apron and busied herself at the sink. "Listen to me croak on. Charles will be home any minute and I must get this placed tidied up."

The mention of my uncle's return made me shudder. I wasn't ready to face him just yet. Grabbing my jacket, I headed for the door.

"It's such a beautiful evening, I think I'll go for a walk up the lake."

Aunt Sophie nodded. "All right. Don't be too late back and remember, you're not allowed to go out in the boat."

"I know," I said as I opened the door and almost collided with Uncle Charles.

"So you're back," he said. "Don't go rushing off on any more mysterious errands. I want to have a word with you."

Reluctantly, I returned to the kitchen and sat at the table. My uncle removed his hat, jacket and boots, washed his hands, kissed his wife perfunctorily on the cheek and joined me.

"What do you think you were doing at the mine this afternoon with that Chinese boy and that radical girl?"

"They are my friends," I replied more loudly than I intended.

Uncle Charles laughed. "You think that, do you? You have a lot to learn about life here. I had hoped you would learn it on your own, using what common sense God gave you, but I see you are not, so I must tell you.

"Back in England, the classes do not mix. A belted Earl will not sit down to dine with a mudlark or a sweep. Can you imagine your grandfather taking port with his gardener?"

My uncle hesitated as if waiting for a reply. My father had talked to me about this very subject on his last leave, about how the community of soldiers in the trenches broke down the social barriers that would have been almost insurmountable in peacetime. How he felt it would not be possible to go back to the same world after the war. Of course, there would still be classes, Field Marshal Haig would not drink beer with a private. Only a revolution like the one in Russia could change that and that was not what father wanted. But he did believe that petty class differences, like the ones that were so important to my grandfather and my uncle, would not be nearly so important after the war that had thrown millions of men together. I didn't say anything.

"Over here, it is just the same," Uncle Charles went on. "The mine owners are a class above the managers, who are a class above the grocers and tradespeople, who are a class above the miners, and all are above the Chinese and Japanese. That is the way it is set up and it works. You will only cause trouble, and get into it, by trying to change that."

"I'm not trying to change anything." I was sounding more annoyed than I should have, but I didn't like being lectured to; I wanted to escape and was scared of the situation I seemed to be in. "I'm just trying to make friends and fit in."

"Maybe, but you are in my charge. If the miners see you hanging around with socialists and Chinese, it undermines my authority at the mine."

"So who am I supposed to hang around with? Jimmy and Morag are the only two people my age in this town who aren't already working down your mine." I heard my voice getting louder but there was nothing I could do about it. Anger was rising in me. It wasn't all at Uncle Charles, it was everything. I could feel all the misery, frustration and loneliness of the past year building up like steam in a boiler ready to explode. My uncle was just the easiest target.

"Am I supposed to sit on my own and count the trees? I didn't ask to come to this God-forsaken place."

"You mind your tongue, boy." Uncle Charles was shouting now, too. His face was red and he held his fists clenched at his side. "You will do as I say while you live in my house. I will not have that socialist rabble at the mine laughing at me because my cheeky little brat of a nephew won't do as he is told."

"Then to hell with living in your house. Maybe *you* are stuck here, but I am not. As soon as possible, I'm gone. I intend to make something of my life. Something that my father would be proud of. If you are happy being some little lord pretending he owns coal mines in the colonies, that's fine, but you are not going to suck me in. I'm going to make my dreams come true."

I thought he was going to hit me then. His face was a mask of rage as he raised his hand and stepped forward. I tensed and closed my eyes, waiting for the blow.

It never fell. Instead, I heard Aunt Sophie's voice. "He's right."

When I opened my eyes, Uncle Charles was still standing in front of me with his fist raised, but he was looking over at Aunt Sophie. She was standing by the sink, her hands still covered in soapsuds. Her eyes were hard.

"If you hit that boy," she said, "I will walk out that door

and never return. God has not seen fit to bless us with children of our own, so I do not know very much about raising them. But I do know that fists are never the answer.

"I also know that the greatest gift we can give a child is the ability to avoid the mistakes we have made. We have made many. You with your unrealistic dreams and me not standing up to them, but I will not stand by and watch you try and crush this boy's dreams. He has been through more than enough without that."

Uncle Charles seemed to collapse. His fist fell to his side and his face sagged visibly. He sat heavily on the chair by the table. Aunt Sophie wiped her hands on her apron and turned to me.

"I think it might be best if you go for that walk now," she said with a faint smile. "Charles and I have some talking to do."

Obediently, I left. I went and sat on the log by the path to try and collect my thoughts. I was close to tears in reaction to the argument with Uncle Charles, but I was also amazed at Aunt Sophie. She had spoken up for me and, I suspected, stood up to her husband for the first time. Life was turning out to be full of surprises.

Since my father died, there had seemed no point in trying to do anything; it was much easier just to drift and let other people make decisions for me. Cumberland had changed that. It was a place that demanded taking sides and making decisions. Every action had a consequence and it was impossible not to become involved. In the emotional roller coaster of the last few days, I had been a part of the racism and ignorance that had killed Jimmy's father, I had found and lost Morag, and I had betrayed Ginger Goodwin. I had not intended for any of it to happen, good or bad, but it had.

The only thing I had had control over was the argument with Uncle Charles and I wasn't very proud of that. It had probably caused all manner of problems between him and Aunt Sophie — just more trouble I had caused. What positive thing could I do to make things better? It was too late for Jimmy's father. Perhaps there would be a time when I could resolve things with Morag, or even my uncle, but it wasn't now. Whatever I had said about Ginger Goodwin in my delirium couldn't be taken back.

Suddenly a thought struck me with the force of a bullet. I sat bolt upright. It was something Morag's father had said to me at the mine, something about keeping both his daughters from running around in the woods tonight. In a blinding flash, I realized what he had meant. He had been giving me a message. Morag wouldn't be going up the lake tonight to deliver the supplies. When I added that to Goodwin's lack of caution, Warren's talk of shooting to kill and finishing it all, and what I had overheard my uncle tell Warren, it was obvious that Goodwin was in mortal danger — unless he was warned, and Morag wouldn't be warning him. That's what her father was telling me. There was no one else to warn Goodwin — no one except me. With the clarity that comes from making a decision, my mind began to work overtime.

First I had to decide how I was going to get down to the far end of the lake. Either I could "borrow" Uncle Charles's boat, or I could walk along the lakeside trails. The former option was much preferable. It would be quicker, easier on my weak ankle, and I would be less likely to get lost. Nights were short at this time of year and the moon would help me navigate. If I travelled overnight, I would be on the Cruikshank well before Warren's posse and I should have plenty of time to warn Goodwin. Disobeying my uncle wasn't a problem any more.

With as much determination as I could muster with my sore ankle, I headed in a wide arc through the trees and around the cabin to the lake shore where the boat was kept.

Uncle Charles kept the oars in the boat, so I was soon out on the water and rowing parallel to the shore. The sun was well behind the trees already, and the water on the lake was dead calm. Insects hummed and buzzed in the still, warm air and tiny concentric ripples appeared as small fish broke the surface to feed. I would have enjoyed myself if I hadn't been so emotionally strung out.

Our cabin was past the mine and the main cluster of dwellings at the bottom of the lake, so I didn't have to row past many other families. The few people I did see merely waved a greeting.

By the time I had found and retrieved Morag's sack of supplies from the eagle tree, the light was fading fast. I rowed until darkness and exhaustion became too much, then I dragged the boat ashore, found some biscuits and got as comfortable as I could.

As I nibbled on the snack, I listened to loons calling eerily over the water and the soft splash of ripples on the shore. A breeze had got up, but it was still warm and there wasn't a cloud in the sky. The stars here looked much bigger and brighter than they did in England. I almost felt as if I could step off the world and fall forever through them. It was very beautiful, but it was a harsh beauty I still wasn't used to, like the huge trees that went on forever or the rugged, unfarmed hills and mountains. Perhaps I could grow to love this place, I thought as I drifted into sleep.

When I awoke, the moon had risen and it was light enough to continue. I rowed slowly, stopping to study the shore for landmarks. Mostly I couldn't see much against the darkness of the forest, but a pale light from behind a cur- tained window showed me where Morag's father's cabin was. I knew he and Morag weren't there, and it was unlikely that Warren had come up this evening. He had talked about setting out the next morning, but other members of his posse might be waiting there.

Eventually, I arrived at the mouth of the Cruikshank River and pulled the boat ashore as far into the trees as I could. There was still some time until daylight, so I hunkered down in the predawn chill and waited.

It seemed hours before the sky lightened in the east and

another eternity before the sun clambered above the trees and brought some warmth to my cold body. At least by then I had formed a plan of sorts. As soon as I had warmed up, I would head up the Cruikshank and leave a warning note at the big rock. Then I would find the trail across the ridge in hopes of meeting Goodwin on his way over.

There were a lot of maybes in it. Maybe Goodwin would use a different route. Maybe he was already camped somewhere down the lake. Maybe I would just miss him in the bush. All I could do was stick to my plan and try. Throwing the sack of supplies over my shoulder, I set off.

Saturday, July 27, 1918

—᙭—

When I reached the post office rock about midmorning, there was no sign that it had been visited since Morag and I were last there. Her note lay untouched where she had left it. Nervous at who might be about, I hurriedly penned a short general warning, removed the supplies from the sack and stacked them as far under the overhang as I could manage. I kept out a few biscuits and some jerky for my lunch.

With the lightened bag, I made good time back to the trail up to the transit camp that we had used in the storm. Going uphill was slower and my ankle became increasingly painful, but I was happy. The weather was beautiful and my climb was occasionally rewarded by stunning views along the lake. At one stop, I even saw a motorboat working its way up the lake and I laughed out loud at how I had out-smarted Warren. My plan was working perfectly. If I didn't meet Goodwin on the trail, all I had to do was wait at the transit camp until he showed up, warn him about the trap and then return home. Perhaps even Morag would forgive me after today.

I was hot, tired and dripping with sweat by the time I reached the camp. It was deserted so I made myself comfortable against a tree and ate the food I had taken from the cache. The dry jerky was hard to chew and I wished I had brought a canteen of water with me, but the food was good and I began to feel drowsy.

I didn't try too hard to stay awake because if Ginger came through the camp he would see me, awake or asleep. I was exhausted and the warm air and humming insects seemed to wrap me in a cocoon of comfort. Nestling down into the soft moss, I was asleep in minutes.

When I awoke, it was late afternoon, about four I judged by the position of the sun. I must have slept for a good three hours at least — and where was Goodwin? No one had come into the clearing and wakened me. With a gnawing worry working its way into me, I picked up the pack, stretched and headed back down the path.

My mouth felt like sandpaper and I had a dull, thumping headache from dehydration. That, and my growing worry, meant that I wasn't paying too much attention when two arms reached out from behind a tree and held me fast. I struggled, but it was no use. Two other figures materialized out of the bush in front of me. Both were dressed in rough work clothes. One carried a fishing rod over his shoulder and the other held a cluster of silver trout by his side.

"Well, what do we have here?" the taller of the two asked.

"I don't rightly know," the other answered, "but I don't reckon it's a fearsome Dominion Constable, so you'd best let him go, Fred."

"Who are you?" I asked as the arms released me.

"Well," the one who had ordered my release said, "I am Arthur Boothman, this here's Jimmy Randall, and you were captured by the mighty Fred Taylor."

I turned my head to see the third man smiling down at me. "And who might you be, young fellow?" he said.

"Will Ryan," I said.

"Ah," Boothman said, attracting my attention back to the front. "The Ryan kid that Ginger saved from the storm last week."

"Where is Ginger?"

"Ah, well now, there's lots of people would like to know that," Boothman said. "Why should I tell you?"

"Because I'm here to warn him."

"Warn him? Of what?"

"Warren knows where his camp is. He has a posse in the woods right now hunting him — and you. Why didn't you come over this trail this morning?"

"This isn't the only trail over this hill. We came around the west end to a fishing hole Ginger knows. But back up a bit. How does Warren know where our camp is?"

I was saved from answering by Fred Taylor pushing past me and joining his companions. "That's no matter. What's important is that Warren does know."

"And how do we know what this lad says is true?" Boothman asked. "His uncle's a boss."

"Did you go to the post office rock?" I asked.

"Yes," Boothman answered uncertainly.

"Well, then you would have found the note I left there and the supplies that Morag was going to bring up but couldn't. It was me who left them there. Why would I do that if I wasn't trying to help?"

The three men looked closely at me for a long minute. "Okay," Boothman said. "So we believe you. Now we have to go and move our camp before Warren gets there. You say he didn't come up this way?"

"No one passed this way today."

"Very well, we might have time.

"Listen, young Will Ryan, will you do us a favour?"

"Yes, if I can."

"Good. Ginger was with us. He stayed down by the Cruikshank to gather blackberries. He's mighty fond of them, but he should be on his way after us now. You go back down the trail and tell him to hurry as fast as those sorry lungs of his will allow. Tell him that, if we've gone from the camp, he's to meet up with us at Hornet Lake. He knows where that is. Have you got that?"

"Yes, Hornet Lake," I said.

"Good. Now get on, we must be moved by dark."

The three men filed past me and headed up the trail. I turned to go down, but Boothman's voice halted me. "Thank you, young Ryan," he said.

I felt important as I headed down the trail — I was making a difference at last — and I was happy. I was going to meet Ginger Goodwin again. Despite the strange circumstances of our last two meetings, I realized now that I liked Ginger. I liked his smile, his ready laugh and his cheeky irreverence for things that other people considered important. Ginger was a lot more like my father than I had been prepared to admit just a few days before. I had learned a lot. I still had a lot of things to work out, but I was much less ready to blame than I had been.

Ginger and I appeared at opposite ends of the small clearing on the trail at the same time. I stepped out of the trees as he came around a rock outcrop about thirty feet ahead of me.

Ginger was hunched forward, eyes on the ground before him, his shoulders rising and falling with his laboured breathing. He was half-turned toward me to negotiate a log, a handkerchief-wrapped bundle of blackberries in his left hand. His hair stood out like a fireball in the low sun.

"Ginger!" I shouted.

He stopped, looked up at me and smiled — then hell broke loose. Ginger raised his bundle in welcome. At the same instant, a figure rose from the undergrowth to Ginger's left and pointed a rifle at my friend.

Ginger froze, his raised arm turned into a gesture of surrender. The world stood still and a strange silence overcame everything. I could hear no sound, no buzzing insect or singing bird, only the rattle of a pebble dislodged by my foot. Eventually it too came to rest.

Incredibly slowly, Ginger turned and looked at the figure pointing the rifle at him. I think in that instant, he saw his fate in Dan Warren's eyes. He turned to look back up at me, the smile still on his lips.

The gunshot shattered the heavy July air, echoing between the towering Douglas firs on the hillside. People as far away as Cumberland claim to have heard that shot. Children splashing in the shallows on the lake shore, women sweeping the porches of their summer cabins, men dressing for another shift down the mine, stopped what they were doing and listened. Perhaps all those who did claim to hear that shot are telling the truth. Perhaps the sound, bouncing off the summer flatness of Comox Lake, did carry incredible distances, but nowhere did that shot sound as loud as it did to me. It was almost a physical thing, hurling itself at me as if it wanted to thrust me back into the hillside.

I have never understood how the tiny movement of a rifle's firing pin igniting a teaspoon of gunpowder can make such a noise — or create such tragedy.

The bullet, soft-nosed and designed to expand on impact to cause maximum damage, did not have far to go. It carved a two inch long gouge in the flesh of Ginger's raised forearm and entered the left side of his neck before it met cartilage and bone and exploded, destroying several vertebrae and severing his spinal chord. Ginger probably didn't even feel the back of his neck being blown out. Robbed of its support, his head lolled ridiculously to one side as his body sagged. Ginger was dead before he hit the ground.

I screamed and leapt forward, scrambling and slithering down the slope, trying to outrun time, to burst back into that moment before the gunshot.

It was hopeless, Ginger's body was still by the time I arrived beside it. In his fall, he had spun around and was lying on his back as if resting, his left leg stretched out down the hill with the other bent beneath it. His right arm lay, twisted awkwardly, under his back. His left arm lay over his stomach, fat blackberries spilling out of his handkerchief. I stumbled forward. Ginger's head was twisted to one side, his hair disheveled and his eyes stared blindly up into the trees. His mouth was open and his gold teeth gleamed. It was as if he were about to make some weighty pronouncement, but he would never speak again. The red stain on his scarf, the spreading pool beneath his head, and the horrible, bottomless hole in his throat told me that. I half-crouched, half-fell forward. My tears poured onto the lapels of his jacket. I had failed. I was too late.

A rough hand grabbed my shoulder and jerked me up

and around. It was Dan Warren. He held a rifle in his free hand.

"What're you doing here?" he asked. I couldn't form answering words through my choking sobs. I just turned my head and looked back at Ginger's body.

"It was him or me," Warren said. "He came upon me sudden. I had to fire first."

Breaking free, I found my voice in a scream. "Liar! Ginger wouldn't have hurt a fly. You murdered him."

"Now wait one minute, Ryan," Warren said. "Red Goodwin was a desperate man. You're but a boy. You don't know what a man like him will do when he's cornered. I know what I saw and I did what I had to do. Don't you go saying otherwise or it'll be the worse for you."

"I know Ginger would never hurt anyone. Even a scab policeman like you."

"Now see here," Warren made another grab for me, but I easily dodged out of his way.

"Murderer! Murderer!" I yelled, pushing through the underbrush and heading back down the hill. I ran blindly, heedless of the branches whipping across my face and the pain in my ankle. My legs could only barely prevent me flying headlong down the slope as they sank into the soft mossy ground. My breath began to come in agonizing gasps and black spots of exhaustion danced in front of my eyes. At last I tripped over a moss-covered log, landed heavily and lay sobbing. Ginger was dead, and it was my fault. I hadn't intended it, but Warren had found him because of me. In that instant I hated myself. And I swore I would never do another thing that could in any way hurt another human being.

That's how Bill Ward found me, sitting against the log, my body wracked by sobs.

"What are you doing here?'" he asked.

I saw my chance for redemption. Ward was a decent man. He would understand and, at least, Warren would be made to pay for his crime.

"Warren murdered Ginger," I blurted out. "He ambushed him up the trail. In cold blood. Ginger was collecting blackberries."

"Calm down. I heard a shot, right enough, so let's go up and see what happened."

Together, we climbed back up to the clearing. Warren was standing over Ginger's body.

"There he is!" I yelled. "He murdered Ginger."

"It was self-defence," Warren said softly.

"No, it wasn't!" I shouted. "It was murder. Ginger was unarmed. He never carried a gun. Warren shot an unarmed man in cold blood. How could it have been self-defence when Ginger wasn't even . . ."

The words stuck in my throat. Sticking out from beneath Ginger's right shoulder and lying accusingly beside his still head, was the steel grey barrel of a .22 calibre hunting rifle. It hadn't been there before, had it? Had I missed seeing it through my tears?

"I surprised him on the trail," Warren said. "I had the

drop on him, but he raised his rifle. I had to shoot. It was him or me."

Now I was certain. Even if Ginger was carrying the gun, he never aimed it at anyone.

"Liar!" I screamed, launching myself at Warren.

He easily thrust me aside. "Now see here. I don't have to justify my doings to some whippersnapper boy. Clear off and let me do what I must. Go on." He raised his hand threateningly.

"What're you going to do?" I spat back at him. "Murder me too?"

For a moment, I thought he was. Warren stepped forward and raised his rifle.

"Stop this!" Ward's voice prevented whatever might have happened. "Dan Warren, you back off. I will not have this boy harmed." Warren retreated and Ward came towards me. "Calm down," he said quietly, "I know this looks bad."

"I know what I saw," I hissed. "It was murder."

Ward sighed. "Even if you are right, it's still only one murder. Thousand's of men are being murdered every day in France. I know. I've seen them die." Ward held up a hand to stop my protest. "I know that doesn't justify what you say you saw here, but it is not up to us. That man," Ward jerked his thumb over his shoulder at Warren, "and the others in the Dominion Police posse, came here to do a job. Word is that next week there is going to be an amnesty for the conscription dodgers."

I looked down at Ginger's body. Was he really that close?

"Not for him," Ward went on. "He's caused too much trouble. Ruffled too many important feathers. There could be no amnesty that included Albert Goodwin. That's why the rush. Goodwin has been doomed ever since he led that smelter strike in Trail. One way or another, they would get him — send him to the meat grinder of the trenches, or hire someone like Warren. There was no way out. There's nothing anyone can do."

"I can say what I saw — that Warren murdered Ginger in cold blood."

"You could, yes. There *will* be an inquiry. But nothing you say will make any difference. It'll be your word against Warren's, and he's a policeman. It's all been decided, you see. You could speak up and make a fuss and a noise, but none of that will change anything. Ginger won't come back and nothing you say will touch Warren. He will tell his version of the story and then disappear back to Victoria, until his unsavoury talents are needed again by the men who never get their hands dirty. Goodwin will be buried and forgotten and life will go on."

"It's not fair," I choked as tears ran down my cheeks.

"No one ever said it was fair," Ward said gently. "I didn't know him well, but I doubt if Ginger Goodwin would have expected fairness."

I looked over at Ginger's body. Already, hungry flies were settling on the thickening pool of blood by his neck.

"Come on, no more jawing," Warren said roughly. "We need to get the hell out of here. Are you going to keep your mouth shut, boy?"

"He won't say anything," Ward said.

"He'd better not, or he'll be sorry."

I wanted to shout and scream at the unfairness of it all. I wanted to grab Warren's rifle and smash it over his skull. I wanted to kick and gouge and tear until Warren felt what it was like to suffer and until my anger was satiated. But I didn't. Instead I turned and walked down the path to the lake.

I wouldn't say anything. They had won. Maybe they would always win, but as I stumbled down that hillside, I heard Ginger's voice echoing through the trees, "you can't win every battle in a war. Just because they win most of them is no reason to surrender. There'll always be another struggle around the corner. The trick is never to give up."

Saturday, January 27, 1968

—⁓—

I once read somewhere that there is a piece of Julius Caesar
in each of us. The idea is that, as Caesar died after being
stabbed two thousand years ago, he let out one final breath.
The molecules of air from that breath spread into the air of
ancient Rome. Enough time has passed for those molecules
to have dispersed completely around the world. Therefore,
everyone alive has breathed in a molecule or two of Caesar's
last breath.

I don't know if it's true or not, but I like to think that
sound works the same way. A loud sound, like a rifle shot,
echoes away until it cannot be heard any more. But perhaps
it goes on echoing, too softly for us to hear except on the

quietest days. Perhaps the rifle shot I heard all those years ago went on echoing: echoing down all the damp, deadly tunnels under Vancouver Island where working men sweated and died digging the coal; echoing through the work camps and the hunger marches of the Great Depression; echoing between the graves of the young Canadians who went and fought in Spain, or France, or Korea. Perhaps it is still echoing along the almost empty streets of the old coal town of Cumberland.

Maybe it is just my fanciful imagination, but the rifle shot that hot afternoon fifty years ago still echoes for me. It marks a divide. Before it I was a child, gloriously ignorant of all complexity and innocent of the evil in this world. After it, I could never be innocent again.

Ward was right about a lot of things. The conscription dodgers were pardoned the following week, there was an inquiry that believed Warren's story of shooting in self-defence and life did go on. But he was wrong about one thing — Ginger Goodwin was not forgotten. On the day of his funeral, the procession of mourners stretched for over a mile and more than five thousand workers in Vancouver downed tools in Canada's first-ever general strike.

The day after the funeral I left Cumberland for ever. The only person who saw me off was Morag. She said that she forgave me, and I never forgot her. I didn't ask her to come with me.

The person I became after that shot echoed around

Comox Lake owes as much to Red Goodwin as it does to my father. As I travelled and learned about the world, I often thought back on all the things Goodwin told me on that cold mountainside after the storm. And the more I thought about it, the more I began to realize he was right — we live our lives as best we can within the limitations of our time and place and the restrictions that powerful men place on us. I have always attempted to live my life, and help my son Ted live his life, in a way that both my father and Ginger Goodwin would be proud of. I hope I have succeeded a little.

The cold gnaws at my bones and my overcoat hangs heavy, laden with the bitter rain. A gust of wind almost knocks me over. Slowly I crouch down, remove some withered stems from Ginger's grave and replace them with the small bunch of flowers I have brought. It's a small gesture, but often that is all we can manage, and someone has to remember.

AUTHOR'S NOTE

—⁓—

Albert "Ginger" Goodwin's life and death are shrouded in mystery, lost records, glorified memories, and outright lies. If you were to collect every scrap of paper containing a concrete, certain fact about him, you would probably not fill a very large shoe box. It's not much for an entire life, but he is still not forgotten.

When the new highway from Nanaimo to Courtenay was opened in 1996, a short stretch that runs beside the old Cumberland cemetery was named "Ginger Goodwin Way" in his honour. Almost the first act after Premier Gordon Campbell's Liberal government took power in 2001 was to tear down the signs with Ginger's name on them. Apparently, Red Goodwin can still raise tempers all these years later.

Red Goodwin is a novel. A novel based on fact but with a lot of my imagination mixed in.

The historical background was taken from two excellent biographies of Goodwin, *Ginger* by Susan Mayse and *Fighting for Dignity: The Ginger Goodwin Story* by Roger Stonebanks. Many evocative historical photographs of the mines, workers and life in general around Cumberland are available for viewing at the Cumberland Museum and Archives.

Ginger did actually walk the streets of Cumberland in 1918 and I have tried to keep my fictional character as close as possible to how the real man might have been. All the other characters are either made up or composites of several real people. Will Ryan has enough imaginative reality to re-appear eighteen years later as Ted's pacifist father in the novel *Lost in Spain.* No historical individual is intended to be truly represented.

I have also taken some liberties with geography, making Comox Lake a bit smaller than it actually is and the wilderness at its north end a bit less forbidding. However, I hope that I have managed to do justice to two things: what life was like in Cumberland in 1918 and the memory of Albert "Ginger" Goodwin.